An Evening in Pisa

An Evening in Pisa

by Pierre Rossi

Translated from the French by Eleanor Levieux

A Howard Greenfeld Book

 J. Philip O'Hara, Inc., Chicago

First published in France under the title
Un Soir à Pise © Flammarion 1971
English text © 1973 by J. Philip O'Hara, Inc.
J. Philip O'Hara, Inc. 20 East Huron, Chicago, 60611.
Published simultaneously in Canada by Van Nostrand
Reinhold Ltd., Scarborough, Ontario.
LC Number: 72-14043
ISBN: 0-87955-902-0
First Printing: D

alla stessa,
in memoria di quella sera.

But what has happened? Everything is so
confused! Why is it suddenly obvious that
someone or something is missing here and that
the music is merely an amusement in the form
of a soliloquy? No one has anything to do.
Is it a wake? Can mourning remain standing
like that? A reception where only the hostess
seems to have been invited. . . There isn't even
anything to expect. Expectation has no role
to play. Everything is there, forever.
No one else has the right to come.

Rainer Maria Rilke

1

"He's late."

"Where is he coming from?"

"And who is he?"

"Our mystery man has got lost on the way," declared Signora Balbi in her sugary voice. "You'll see, he'll have gotten it mixed up, he'll have gone to the Nettuno ballroom next door, to wind up his evening. And when I say, to the ballroom. . .Did somebody draw him a diagram, at least? He has just arrived from Pisa; right on her heels, apparently." And, as no one was paying any attention: "That will make one more dancer," she sighed.

Constantly threading into the blurred laughter of this fashionable reception came the chords of a faraway music, domineering and—to put it frankly—disagreeable; organ music; a church hymn; a refrain repeated with imperceptible variations: *Tuba mirum spargens sonum per silentia regionum.* Dreary and dirgelike, the harmonies developed too vast a universe of sound. "Personally," said Antella, "music makes me sad, as if my heart were in mourning. It would be so nice of your husband to come and join us, instead of shutting himself up like a bear with that keyboard of his. He's become so unsociable!" and, leaning toward Pia's ear, she murmured something to her that made her blush.

"Is he a new lover? Tell us about him, Pia, come, sit here. Tell us about him. . .She doesn't want to; she won't answer. See, I've guessed right. He's in love with her."

"But the whole town is already in love with you, Pia. Leave us the foreigners at least. Let us be loved a little too."

"I think I know what he's like. He has a head like a gladiator, and beautiful teeth. I saw him strolling along the Arno by himself. In this country only foreigners will take their loneliness out for a walk like that."

"A gladiator? What's that?"

"Someone very wicked, at any rate; but with Pia, he'll find it hard going."

The archpriest, already asleep on his feet, was hardly listening to the lean lawyer: "OK as far as the duties of the Church are concerned, Father. But just you explain this marriage to me. She is so young, so pure, sprightly as a kid and—allow me—so delectable. As for him—he's a madman; that disturbing head, those eyes, hot enough to burn your soul; indecency made man. Have you ever seen him smile? A real slash of the razor. The last time he had me come to his property in Orcino for a deed of sale, he was wearing a cat's fur vest, all claws bared. And a woman-chaser to boot. Who ever had the idea of marrying a tomcat like that to such a baby kid? Why not give her back her freedom?"

There was a pause which made the tumult of the organ still more unbearable as its echoes rebounded from the gilt surfaces of the salon. Here and there heads bowed, the better to listen: *Tuba mirum spargens sonum per sepulcra regionum.* . .The master of the house made such peculiar jokes. Who would ever think of drowning one's guests in thundering dirges?

"Her freedom? But she doesn't ask for it," the priest replied. "And what would she do with it? Fall right into the beaks of certain birds of prey I happen to know? What the Church upholds in a marriage, my friend, is not the happiness of the couple but their union; it's the institution which the Church wants to save, not the partners in it. And how do you know, after all; perhaps that child is very happy. Just look at her."

"I love being sad, it does me good," meditated a long-haired damsel aloud. "At least you feel your heart living. Suppose we dance."

"Look at that, there's Vana about to cry. Open the window, it's stifling in here."

"Tell me, Chiarina, was it you who taught our Pia to be so beautiful? How elegant she is tonight!"

"Come now, can you see me as a professor of beauty! You know very well our Pia won't let anyone teach her anything. Someone as proud as she is?. . .I told her it would be folly to wear that dress; she would look just too overdone. Brocade on brocade, a doll from the costume museum. She bought it anyhow and kept on saying, over and over, "Splendid! Splendid! Chiarina, I want to be covered with flowers like a meadow, like our *camposanto.*" Well, it's true! On her, those seed-beds of flowers have come alive: look at her. You know why you find her so beautiful? I'll tell you why: because she doesn't talk. She cries (if you only knew how much she cries!), she sings, she laughs, but she talks so little. She says she hasn't the time. She's out of breath from living. She is from Siena, and she is coquettish and secretive like all Siennese women."

"Just enough sadness for a great love," said a man

who was dancing.

"You know perfectly well she thinks only of herself. An egoist, that's all. She doesn't love anyone. Oh look! Who's that?"

He had just entered the great hall, called the Hall of Angels, where this reception was taking place. In the old city of Pisa, most of the noble residences were historied like that, with labels put on everything from the cellar to the rafters. The crystal chandeliers had been lighted. People crowded the room, even the walls of it: for on a level with a man's head was another floor of trompe-l'oeil marquetry work where, as far as the eye could see along a perspective of corridors, dogmatic figures with pointed noses and waxen faces, who wore the long togas of confessors, stood before open antiphonaries on enigmatic tablatures. Above, alternating with oval mirrors set deeply into dark wood panels and set off by candelabra, stretched a frieze of painted riverscapes, dimmed with blue, like the sky over Nimwegen.

He saw her. She was emerging from one of those illusive galleries next to an allegorical doctor drawn in red chalk, whose motionless eye seemed to stare at that magnificent prey: aloe-colored gown bedizened with immortelles; beautiful, more than beautiful! From the bare shoulders seemed to flow an ascensional move-

13

ment, as in Titian's *Assunta,* in mid-sky; the wide burning mouth, the spacious forehead, the robust surfaces of the face where the shadows placed multiple temptations, everything about her sought a relationship with this world full of angels on the threshold of which she appeared.

"At last," he said, "I have found you again. . ."

With a gesture of impatience at the ever-disturbing noise of the organ, she continued to come toward him. At her side, on a console table, gleamed fruits and small carafes; against her shoulder opened a tableau where, in very clear weather, lines of willows and pomegranate trees could be seen unfurling, composing a backdrop of superimposed horizons.

"We were not expecting you any more," she said, "except me. I know how faithful you are."

"At last," he repeated. "Good evening to you. Thank you for your invitation. What victory are you celebrating today? All this glory around you, and that music, so solemn. . ."

"An anniversary: my wedding anniversary. I wanted you so much to be with us. Chiarina, Vana, Antella, and you, dear Father, come, let me introduce our French friend. He wants to apologize for arriving late."

Introducing them, she had that merciful air of hers,

14

that air of moving forward through great fatigues. And he watched her, as filled with wonder as on the first day, with the same questioning, the same waiting, a feeling of having come to another country once and for all. Through the clear organdy he could see a heavy pectoral cross, incrusted with garnets, plunging into the cleft of the breasts and held back by a slender twist of emerald-colored silk around the strong neck. Although he guessed the innermost life of that bosom, it barely moved with her breathing.

Once again he saw the landscape by the Atlantic where he had met her for the first time, last summer, in that little city where, accompanied by Chiarina, she had come as a tourist to buy laces.

"Goodbye for now," she had called from the window of the compartment. "Goodbye for now. Remember the invitation. Yes, yes, you'll see how pleasant the autumn is in Pisa; from October to April, only one day of snow."

Yes, it was by the Atlantic. He had asked to talk with her again, alone, the day before she was to leave; she had refused. He had had to accept Chiarina's presence. So they had met in a café and exchanged futile words constantly interrupted by the chatter of Chiarina, eager to go home "to do the packing," "to have Madame rest before the long trip," "to go have a last look at the shop windows." And while Pia soothed the impatient, gossiping Chiarina by placing her hand on her knee, she held her gaze in that of the man, reserved and attentive.

But long before, there had been their first meeting, under circumstances which remained uncertain; it had come about by chance. No one had introduced them to one another; things had happened much more naturally—that is, much more strangely—than that. It was a public place where they hadn't much room, they had talked about this and that, Chiarina had been present, then they had gone out, all three together.

The thought of her had not left him since. He had followed her like a shadow, compelling himself to see her again every day, every day more fascinated. She was so much more vivid than the others despite her indolent voice. She was so new. So he had worn himself out trying to win her, to convince her:

"I have found you at last. . ."

"You do not know me."

"I will keep on looking for you."

"You haven't the right."

"Be quiet, give me your lips."

"No."

"Stay, don't leave again."

"But I cannot. . ."

"Where do you live? Tell me. I will go there."

"Child!"

Out of lassitude, playfulness perhaps, in one of those anonymous and ever-green gardens along the Atlantic, she had finally ceded him a brief kiss that was both smiling and cold. But those lips—it was as if he had not touched them; they were but a drawing in that face which never ceased to flee, to veil itself, look elsewhere.

"Lungua guerra de'sospiri!" she concluded, in her deep Tuscan voice.

Just as inexplicably she had asked him to come to the station to witness her departure; she had invited him to make the trip to Pisa, if he had the time; it would amuse her to see him again; it would make her happy; she insisted on it, at all costs.

"Goodbye for now!" she had cried from the door of the train. "Goodbye for now! Remember, I'll be expecting you. You'll see how pleasant the autumn is in Pisa. . ."

Several weeks later, he had received a formal invitation by which "Signor and Signora dei Tolomei begged him to attend their annual reception." With it came a short note signed Niccolo, insisting that it would be a pleasure to receive him.

Now, in this hall where the chandeliers and the mirrors gleamed, he was in a dream. He had found her again. Nothing was unlooked-for, since she was there. Joyously she had just clasped both his hands, as if they had said goodbye only the day before:

"Isn't it true that you are going to apologize for having made me wait?"

"Pia, Pia! Listen! Your husband is going to come. The music has stopped."

A hush had just fallen over the salons, which suddenly seemed deserted. The organ was still. Everyone felt abandoned below the monumental ceiling streaked with trumpets and astir with Latin streamers, opening here and there onto blue-painted skies, fresh as vents of open air.

"We're going to surprise him. Come on, everyone in front of the musician's door, lined up, like an honorary review. La Pia will go to meet her husband and they will kiss in front of the people."

"When it comes to kissing, he'll kiss all right," the archpriest grumbled in a murmur.

Arm in arm, they danced into line on the threshold of the low door; through the opening they could see the angular perspective of another room, a *studiolo* on whose multicolored tile floor the furtive light cut out

18

bevelled marble edges. What steps were going to move over those glazed surfaces? What shadow would be cast on them? What could he be like, this man he did not know and who had married Pia, who loved her, took her in his arms, in his bed, every evening; on whom she fell silent.

"When he comes through the doorway, we must all cry out together, *Viva l'Amore!* Otherwise, watch out, Niccolo loves only love."

They exchanged knowing smiles. Pia had checked the reflection of her hair in the back of a silver dish, then had crossed her hands and stretched both her arms, which she now swung at her sides. He was embarrassed. He felt sorry he had come, sorry he had been caught up in such company. But time passed; the guests grew impatient; the music had not started again, yet no one appeared in the entrance to the hall.

"It would seem he isn't there any more," someone murmured.

"With him, anything is possible; he plays a magician's pranks."

"What's he holding in store for us now?"

"Suppose I go and get him. . ."

Then it was that they heard, on the bridge, the gallop of a horse and a calash rattling away. They were disconcerted. Some of them shrugged their shoulders. Two windows were opened. Into all the rooms, now being emptied of their guests, came the coolness of the air and the trickling of the Arno which bathed the throng of mural angels, more motionless than ever.

Shivering, wrapping her long hands about her shoulders, she turned to him. "You see," she said, "it is autumn."

2

Night had now invaded the city of the Ghibellines. The guests had departed and behind them, on the paving stones of the alleys, echoed—not their voices, but the sound of their high heels striking the night like clicking dice.

"But where is he?"

"Who?"

"Your husband, of course. Didn't you invite me to your wedding anniversary? You are the bride; but where is the bridegroom?"

"He's flown away, disappeared, and at a gallop, too."

The last white-haired, amaranth-jacketed servant had gone from drawing room to drawing room, precautious and attentive as if he had forgotten something or was looking for something that others might have forgotten; step by step he had extinguished the chandeliers, blown

21

out the coppices of candles that had been placed on the pedestal tables. He had withdrawn at last, backing out and gratifying him, lord knows why, with the title of "Excellency." Upstairs, Chiarina was readying the bed chambers; she could be heard rummaging about.

Leaning on their elbows at the window overarched by a vault of reddish brick, they listened to the Arno flee under the Ponte di Mezzo. From it a very light fog lifted, whose white shadows mingled with the background of cool air; long leafless trees, stiff in a decorative way, helped to make the grassless terrace along the Galileo embankment barer still. The south wind lighted them.

She smiled, pointed toward the landscape, and on her face appeared that marvelous incredulity she had shown on certain days by the Atlantic.

"If you had come in the summertime, I would have taken you to listen to the crickets of Ansedonia. But you have come too late; you always come too late."

"You know very well it is not I who chose the time of my coming; let's postpone the crickets until next year. I prefer you to them, I swear I do."

"How do they manage to be so happy? To go on singing for weeks and weeks? None of us poor humans can do that."

22

Once again making the familiar gesture of half-veiling her face with her scarf, she simulated anxiety:

"Do you still love me as much?" she murmured, in that Saracen way of hers.

"Close your eyes, give me your lips, and you'll see."

"No, speak softly. Chiarina might hear. She would tell everything. She mustn't."

"You are so beautiful. . ."

"It is only because you are thinking of me that I am beautiful, because you want me."

"Yes, I do want you, every day, every hour, unceasingly. I need you, I need you. The blood I can feel rising to your cheeks, belongs to me. . ."

"Don't ever say that again; I'm afraid. . ."

She had backed away, keeping herself at a distance once more; she was far away again. She smiled at his hesitant Italian; at times, it did not ring true. For instance, he would say "balconu" for *finestra* and, more oddly still, "riguardare" for *guardare*. All in all, she spoke French better than he spoke Italian.

"I have come only for you and yet if there is one thing I am growing certain of, it is this: pursuing you forever, I will never reach you."

"Do you believe that?"

She showed him the diamond wedding band around

her finger.

"How could I give myself? Nothing belongs to me, not even myself. Do you believe in hell? I do. Leave, leave before I do you a great deal of harm."

"Not before I have told you that I love you. Let me repeat it; let me go with you through the gates of your delightful hell."

"Hush! You mustn't. No, don't look at me so meaningfully; not today; it is not allowed."

"When then?"

"One day. . ."

"Soon?"

"Do not ask. I have met you too late. There was a time when I also lived free. Where were you then? You have wasted too much time along the way, loitered too much before other people's doors."

"You keep running from me."

"No no, I am staying; here, take my hand. Only do not demand of me what I cannot give you. Be my friend. After all, have I asked you who you were? I am superstitious and your heart is so curious that I do not wish to lose it."

She went on, "Goodbye for now, good night. You will be staying in Pisa for a while, won't you? We will see each other again. Do not be sad. Yes, yes, Chiarina, I am coming."

3

"No matter how you look at it, it's a strange thing to do, leave your guests for the sake of a dog," said Isidoro Falchi, the coachman, to himself. "He does things no one else would do; oh, a fine dog, all right but still, his wife, his friends, his anniversary. . ."

"By the time we get there, Sigismondo will be dead," Niccolo dei Tolomei was thinking, unmercifully jostled by the jolting cabriolet. The road that led to the Orcino farm was nothing more than broken stones between walls of tuff with a few withering clumps of asphodel and fennel. Cars fell to pieces on it, and he had preferred to trust Isidoro's old cabriolet. A real martyrdom. During the daytime at least there were the circling buzzards, that bawled above the brambles, to liven the landscape. But at night all that remained were the heavy square rocks, the mute hillsides, a compact land unable to breathe. Firmly, Isidoro held the reins which cut into his hands. Bent over his seat like a kingfisher, he tried to discipline his physiognomy into that high-class boredom he admired on his master's face, the arrogance of people who believe the entire world is subject to their will. Even Niccolo's laconic manner impressed him so that his lips had puckered in that peculiar way you see on the mouths of the mute.

The weather and the sky were astonishing. The moonlight, broad and pure, struck the rump of the sweating mule like spinning snow and polished the brass harness nails. Inside his carapace of leather and moon, the animal moved like a crustacean, the rump swinging in the middle of a calm landscape, ravaged by torrents of sand. Beneath a barely perceptible wind with an aftertaste of mint, the night air had a burnt smell. It was the season for cleaning the fields. The remains of great grass fires, greenish trails of smoke, still crawled along the banks cut out of the chalk until they grew colorless and were extinguished by the heavy, scattered cypress trees, tan with moon dust.

No point in cracking the whip. The mule would go no faster; an invincible hostile current hobbled his legs. Every time he stumbled, one wheel of the cabriolet rose up, hung in mid-air, leaned over, broke a pebble into gleaming fragments, cast a dipping shadow stretched with black spokes which vanished upward to merge, one by one, with the summit of a cypress, a sharp-pointed equinoctial star between two clouds.

"If only I get there in time," said Niccolo dei Tolomei to himself. "Those fools might put him out of his misery. A dog like that! He's worth ten of them, a beast that could teach them a thing or two." Isidoro, for his part, kept quiet. He knew how furious the master was at the accident that had happened to his favorite dog, the Carpathian greyhound he had paid so much for last year at the San Antioco market. Hastily he had left behind friends, wife and guests and run to be with Sigismondo. A strange man, that Niccolo dei Tolomei! He knew how to talk to you, he was even generous, prodigal, with pockets as big as the well of San Patrizio; but haughty, opaque, with something spectral about the cut and the color of his clothes. Solitary, yes, but lover-like as a cat; oh, an aristocrat all right, where that was concerned. Chiarina herself, although she was almost a dwarf. . .and who could say? maybe Isidoro's own wife. . .Didn't they call him "the snake-charmer"? He was too well dressed, too stiffly. Nasty for sure. Not the clumsy, vulgar barefaced nastiness you find everywhere. Isidoro sensed a pomp-and-circumstance nastiness clothed in benevolence, embellished by the stellar brilliance of Niccolo's eyes, a brilliance which seemed to dim the light around him and which Isidoro admired. A nastiness beyond evil, for which there could be no redeemer, no savior; a most sumptuous, most serene nastiness, and before it, Isidoro's recriminations or reasonings crumpled till they were like those oven-dried mintleaves that Niccolo's hands reduced to powder in his teacup. A devil of an aristocrat!

A man dressed in corduroy rode by them on a large Maremma mule. He had a hoe over his shoulder and was on his way to stand his watch over the irrigation sluices. He went by without greeting them. As soon as the first lights appeared, shrill cries pierced the night. It was the madwoman, sequestered in an attic for years, behind a mullioned window. Day and night she played at catching the branches of a mulberry tree close by. Every time she succeeded, she gave a howl of triumph.

So they entered the farm at Orcino, amid the acclamations of the madwoman. A postern gate, a rectangular courtyard where two saddled horses were tied up (Isidoro recognized the roan, belonging to old Paganelli, the veterinarian), a low wall that bore coats of arms here and there and bristled with iron blades, two pilasters, a second courtyard with a short flagged drive; on a level with it, in the middle, the master's house:

four yellow doors under an arcade, set in a freshly whitewashed wall with projecting bosses from which heavy creepers drooped. In the meadow daisies grew in tufts, like gorse. Down to the edges of two pools prickly with long metallic-spiked grasses stretched alternate masses of black and white. These were sleeping sheep.

The whole sight was so reminiscent of a wake for a dying man that one expected to see a priest. Furtively, people came and went; a dozen in all; neighbors; men only, no women, as always here on important occasions.

"Well now, what's happened?" shouted Niccolo. He jumped out of the cabriolet. One of the farmers, skinny as a spider, explained to him, with scythe-like gestures, how a harrow had ripped open the flank of the handsome Carpathian dog—"a wound so deep you could put your hand inside it." Paganelli had sewed him up but the animal was dying. They had stretched him out in front of the fireplace, on a bread board, the kind that is used in certain parts of rural Tuscany when a peasant woman is in labor: it is cleaner and easier to handle than a bed.

With his back to the fire, the veterinarian shrugged his shoulders when he saw Niccolo come in; he spread his hands and shook his head to show that there was no hope. Niccolo knelt and leaned over the greyhound, stretched full length on his left flank; through the transparent cloth bandages, the hemorrhage was visible. The blood was draining out of the magnificent animal. The straw they had slipped under the board was becoming sticky with a purplish mud.

The broad, streamlined chest, capable of sustaining great leaps, was beginning to sag under the weight of death. The elastic power of the thighs, the firmly adjusted dorsal muscles which, when tensed, constituted a mechanism for victory, relaxed, then abruptly, spasmodically, stiffened fit to crack the skin; then the eyelids lifted in flaring wrath; a hurricane seemed to rage in the phosphorescent networks of the capillaries, colored by floral ramifications; yet no dread was mingled there, only an intense fever, a cry of blood shot with purple, with violet, with all the shades of the spectrum. This anatomy designed to storm the open air was trembling at the storm of impending shipwreck, without a moan, without a tear.

Niccolo thought what a sad sight had been the deaths of his father, first, then of his first wife, with so many death-rattles, so many doctor-executioners, so many confessions, so much vehemence, only to end in the ultimate, moralizing secret consultations and the absurd appeal, by a poor little village priest, to the souls of people who had long before ceased having souls to save or to lose. How different from Sigismondo's solitary elegance! He at least demonstrated to the very end his imperious right to live, with ears back, belly taut, throat tight for the struggle, one more struggle among so many others, the teeth clean with the sharp trenchant whiteness of icicles. In their last hour, the noses of Niccolo's father and grandfather had become discolored, appearing full of hairs and snot. Whereas Sigismondo's muzzle remained as delicate and sensitive as it had been, only yesterday, in the sweet-smelling hay of the hills; at its tip, a palpitation stirred by the very warm odor of the resinous wood which flamed in the hearth. His suffering was traversed by a current of bracing scent; radiant whiffs of this intoxication wafted to the very depths of his agony. So the poison of death and the pleasure of spring produced physical effects that were identical, since both made the animal feel the same painful surprise, the same startled leap of the veins—toward what rebellion, toward what hopes?

Wondrous nature! Uninterrupted mystery of creation! Niccolo laid his cheek against the head of his companion of the wide-open spaces, and the smell of his coat reminded him of the smell of the mastic-trees along the winding banks of the river Orcino, the smell of drumming rain, the smell of the wind gathering the tones of dawn, the smell of noontime sleep that brings overwhelming well-being, after the hunt, during a pause in the ploughing.

What a vigorous, what an admirable agony! Yes, it would last a long time, that agony would; for Sigismondo, to combat the inexplicable shadow that was closing in, disposed of incalculable sources of strength enclosed within him: concentrated rays of the suns of each season, atoms exhaled by the plants, the water, the minerals; in the course of his adventures with the earth from the Carpathians to Tuscany, he had gathered the aromas which vitalize; he knew the mood of the stars; far better than deafened men, he knew the secret pace of Hecate; he was capable of judging the weaknesses of it, capable even of halting its fatality. Niccolo, on the day of his death, would certainly give a great deal to possess Sigismondo's secrets, his lofty valor, his silence. For Sigismondo did not capitulate; with his nails he clung to the earthly paradise, the only one he knew, whose reflection developed within him in the form of desire, of a magnificent interior image, doubtless immortal and so much less artificial than that vague thing which men called their soul, their hèart, their love. . .

"A valiant, insolent creature, this Sigismondo, a virtuoso," thought Niccolo; "a tall wave, that will remain a wave as long as there is a breath to raise it up. Once that godlike breathing, come from god knows where, has expired, the wave will spread itself even with the universal sea and seem to annihilate itself, but only to be reborn another day, farther away, in the form of another wave, as soon as the breeze that suits it has risen again. In this way the valiant are freed of the fear of annihilation and admitted into the endless round of metamorphoses which, in the last analysis, are merely the alternating persistence of similitudes. That is how the valiant live, without fear or hope."

Niccolo smiled briefly as he noted that the dog was dying under the sandalwood and ivory crucifix brought back from Jerusalem by a pious neighbor. And after all, why wouldn't Christ's gaze turn toward this sinless creature that had also, in its own way, so often celebrated the glory of the Creator? Ah, how instructive had been the last time Sigismondo had gone out hunting! There they were, on horseback, he Niccolo, his three colossal neighbors, the one from Santa Riparata, the one from Fragola, the one from Sagona and la Cirnaca, with their three purplish faces; the shepherds, the ridiculous valets in their coral jerkins with the

33

unmatching buttons. And those huntress wives, how pitiful! got up in sports duds straight out of the "hunting goods" department of Tortola and Co.'s store, real frights with all that make-up, smoking cigarette upon cigarette and choking, coughing, holding their stomachs as they sat in their saddles; and you should have seen their horses, as disguised as they were, braided, bedizened, beribboned; real whores, those horses were. And as the hunting horns clashed, all of them, horsemen and horsewomen, full of *zamponi* and *mozarella,* rushed to the assassination of a pale and terrified fox cub hardly bigger than a squirrel. Opened wide to the light of the Tuscan sky, the flowered foliage of the forest watched their carnival mob go by, swelled and animated by the puerile joy of cornering a ludicrous prey, eager to come together soon, at nightfall, in the indulgent hunting lodge, where men and women, mingling, would exchange their sweat. Only the dogs, light as birds, indefatigable and disinterested, contributed a spiritual note to this idiotic concert. Sigismondo was the proudest of them all; you should have seen how majestically his royal whiteness flew over the olive-green undergrowth. How could the Creator, if he existed, have preferred the folly of that disenchanted human horde to the grace of Sigismondo? Yes, it was only right that the Jerusalem crucifix should hover over his agony.

"Master Paganelli, are you really sure there is nothing to be done?" asked Niccolo. The veterinarian did not answer. The farmers who were there, all hunters, understood Niccolo's sorrow. They whispered as if at mass. They too cared about their dogs, sometimes more than about their wives: stiff-spined, hairy-chested, with their dancing walk, their large taciturn eyes that had no iris, their hard teeth for biting but also for answering a smile without seeking it, they were peasants with noggins hard as wood. Niccolo detested the dandies, the artists, the pun-makers, those brainless comedians who prowled around Pia and around their drawing room (for instance, that foreigner, invited just recently). Italy, his Italy, meant these simple country men, swift as greyhounds, eternally sure of themselves, taking themselves for God the father, lovers, not suitors, insolent, not penitent: real dogs.

"Well, Paganelli, you give up?"

"It will be all over soon," said a peasant, placing the palm of his broad hand on the animal's flank. "We've dug his grave over toward the swamp. He'll be comfortable there." The blood had stopped oozing from the stiffened bandage. A pulpy spittle overflowed the beast's jaw; a sort of cloud passed suddenly over his coat, dimming the sheen of it, until then clear and polished by the fire. The paws untensed; the earth was leaving him already; scales of clay flaked off the nails; the eyelids took on hues of blue and black. Sigismondo was beginning his ascension toward the equinoctial stars. The hound's wrath was assuaged and he conceived a great compassion for the life which was ebbing from him. He became quiet and gentle. He had forgiven death.

Above him the men had gathered. Their heads touched. In the half-light they looked like a group of horses standing over the drinking trough. The animal's breathing, between his palate and his teeth, echoed like flowing water interrupted by obstacles of stone. Impossible not to hear it emerging from those backs bent over him. When it took on a deeper resonance, they knew the end had come.

"We must make him beautiful," said Niccolo, clapping his hands. Almost immediately one of the men present disappeared and came back with Gaetana who carried, on her forearms, a majolica basin filled with hot water and, between her teeth, a package of cotton. Slowly, applying himself, Niccolo laid out the body. He washed the soiled muzzle, wiped away the humors from the eyes with their curving lashes. By his side the girl helped him, holding out the basin; her back was arched, her shoulders thrown back, her mass of humid black hair, thick as plumage, held on the nape by a green lace. Notwithstanding the season, she was barefoot and her broad toes stuck out from the sleeveless black shift she used as a nightgown. She had just been awakened. Rustically built, still heavy with sleep, she had to make an effort to remain standing on her full-heeled feet; tight-grained, without an instep, they were made to support the weight of a statue. The brown of her skin had the consistency and the porous tonality of what the colorists call terra cotta. A fine strapping girl, this Gaetana, primitive like Sigismondo. How old was she? Let's see: fifteen? sixteen? Niccolo tried to remember the exact year in which she had come into the world. Who knows, maybe she had been "picked" from her mother's womb, as they say here, on the very board where the hound's cadaver now lay. Fraternity, identity of birth and death! So Niccolo's gaze went from the dog to the girl. By a mysterious transfer, the paradisiac forces which had just abandoned Sigismondo were carried over to this young human body with its surprising carnal density, that had bloomed from contacts with the fieldgrasses and the siliceous dust of the countryside. For the first time Niccolo admired Gaetana, with her face as smooth as a tobacco leaf and the lips authoritarian and new.

The dog did not move any more. "Now he will be able to sleep," she said tranquilly, a shade reproachfully, and put down on the floor the basin in which blood-soaked wads of cotton floated. Then the men took the cadaver and went out, muttering a quick good night.

When Gaetana moved to follow them in turn, Niccolo held her back by the hand. They looked at each other. Her eyes were between gray and black, sad but without fear or care. Never before had she entered this seignorial hall and there come face to face with the man they called the master. She inspected the walls. Niccolo, who had sat down, did not take his eyes off her. In the room were three oil paintings, moderately well varnished. This one she knew; that must be San Donnino walking along briskly, decapitated, his head in his hands. Peculiar, the one over there: a very tall, slightly bony woman with a graceful face, dressed in the Rhenish fashion, her right hand on a gospel-book: Niccolo's first wife, who had died of despair or paludism, they said, probably both, on a farm in the maremma where her husband had relegated her: why? No one knew exactly but he himself had not seemed unhappy when she passed away, and his marriage with Pia had come very soon after the Rhenish woman was buried. Lastly, a large portrait of a sulky child, in tight silk clothes, a flower in his fingers, a whip about his neck. "Who is that?" she asked. "Me, of course; don't you know?" said Niccolo, pulling her to him by both arms. She came forward, unthinking, her face unchanging, opening into Niccolo's eyes the great wind of her dilated pupils. In a sole attempt at self-defense, her two hands, fingers outspread, pressed against her swollen breasts at the same time as a challenging smile lifted the corner of her lips.

Niccolo drew her to him. He placed a kiss on each hand, placed his cheek against the taut, barely rounded belly, whose palpitation filled the universe. Like the branches of a grove, Gaetana's legs opened. In one stride, he closed the door and took out the key. The two of them slipped down onto the fur spread before the hearth. She hadn't even time to take off her dress, the same fire caught them, he ardent as when hunting, she drowsy in the hollow of the swell that was carrying her away. She felt herself transformed into a landscape from which arose the scents of beaten bushes; her mouth took on the iodated taste of that Ischian white wine, *epomeo*.

"Look at me," she said.

"Why do you want me to look at you?"

"So that I'll belong to you."

The ochre of the hills, the azure of San Damiano visible above the mule-drivers' shoulders, the chestnut trees of the Val d'Orezza when the August wind calls them, all of this sprang from the curves and the coombs in which Gaetana's nudity was shaped.

"Does it hurt you?"

"No, it's good, it's good. Again."

In the shadow of her loosened hair, he saw the haystack of the Vasparu meadow; from Gaetana's bosom raced the herd of horses at Orcino, their manes floating as they leaped, silhouetted against the light, against the piles of the bridge, haunches striped and glossy. Haystacks, tight-flying thrushes, shallow rivers, head winds and slanting winds, Gaetana was all that. Arched high, lifting him on a slow and anxious rhythm, she breathed a desire for open air, spilled over with life of which he was the creator. Their veins, their arteries, their nerves, meshed in a single sheaf, composed a sweetness that squeezed their vertebrae so hard as to make them cry. From his mouth she drank the breath of the forest. She cried out, pushing him away,

"No, I don't love you any more," she moaned.

"I don't need to have you love me."

Lucid, aloof from the way Gaetana was carried away, he took his pleasure in measuring the power he held to excite an adolescent's sensitivity.

In weary detachment they grew calm at last. Gaetana's brow became smooth again; on her lips the taste of tears faded. She said, "I am so sleepy," then in an arid voice, resuming her ordinary life, she began to hum a popular song from the coastland, *Torna a Sorriento*... How small she had become again! Stretched out on her back, her head resting on her loosened hair that was plum-colored now in the darker night, her ankles close together and the black dress pulled down over them, she had a monastic look. In her he was witnessing the fulfilment of what people call a soul and which is doubtless nothing more than the coursing of blood, the peacefulness of the soul being explicable only by the happiness of the blood. Thanks to Gaetana, Niccolo this evening could take himself for the Creator.

He was sometimes visited by this sort of peace in church when, the priest and the persons serving mass, supernaturalized in their gold and ruby raiment, moved gravely below the protective gestures of a host of multi-colored saints, archangels and apostles, during the *Magnificat* by Claudio Monteverdi, a musician he revered. But that sort of peace too was obtained through the glorification of the senses, the lustfulness of hearing and sight, the full blossoming of the body, not its mortification.

This evening, the silence and tranquillity of his senses coupled in his memory the savor of Gaetana's body and the glory of church hymns. He himself had played the *Gloriosi corporis misterium* on the organ so often that he could not imagine a more perfect harmony than the embrace of two lovers surrounded by the strains of liturgical music. Hadn't Pia joined him one Sunday up there in the organ loft? on the day of a parish high mass, with flowers fastened in sprays, solitary lilies, garlands of fern woven into arches from pillar to pillar, flowered candelabra distilling fruity scents. Horrified, she had defended herself, doing the sign of the cross as he kissed her, but her shame made her decidedly too tempting; he had taken her, on the threshold of the allegorical paradise painted on the vaulted cathedral ceiling. In the end she gave herself up with the resignation of a martyr or a profaned communion wafer. The organ had fallen silent all of a sudden and the throng below, startled, surmised that the organist had had an attack, while only the monochord voice of the officiant survived in the silence of the *Mea maxima culpa* and the choir boys, wearied by the long ceremony, exchanged sighs.

Since then Pia had been in both agony and delight over this mortal sin committed right in front of God. He knew she wondered whether he was not the devil incarnate. But he refrained from revealing to her that what she considered scandalous, ordinary people merely thought a good idea; that more than once, in the shadows of the duomo in Pisa, or even under the street lamps of their worm-eaten parish of Orcino, he had come across modest provincial lovers, just as swooning, just as triumphant. Not to mention the bygone days, the reputation of the Madonna del Orto for instance, in the northern, downfallen district of Venice, whose discreet walled gardens, planted by the *procuratore* of Saint Mark's in person, Thomas Contarini, own brother to that illustrious Cardinal Gaspard, sheltered the rendezvous of adorers of profane sensual pleasures, clerics and laymen alike. The tradition was being perpetuated: *Magnificat anima mea corpus tuum. . .*

Gaetana had fallen asleep, despite the hardness of the floor through the fur, and the fire in the fireplace had gone out. Then for a long moment everything ceased to move, as if the sky had come down to the earth or the earth had hoisted itself up to meet the sky. Gaetana's bosom rose regularly between those two universes made one. Then it became so oppressive that the sleeping girl started:

"What is that?" she murmured.

"What?"

"That, that noise."

"That noise? That's the silence."

He did not see her any more. From under the door he could hear the muffled steps of his peasants coming back from burying Sigismondo, who had been returned to the warm womb of his mother the earth.

4

"Three crazy women, that's what you are!" laughed
Pia, hands clasping her knee as she talked. "Three crazy
women," she repeated. There they were, on this
October afternoon—Chiarina, old Magia and Maria
Antonia the peddler-woman, kneeling before a flat satin
and bamboo embroidery basket filled with frilly things.
They knew that Pia adored dainty lingerie and, to tempt
her, the three of them had just murmured some
disturbing allusions to the all-powerful charms of
feminine negligees. "No, don't talk about that,
especially not on a Sunday," protested squire Tolomei's
wife, sulking ever so slightly, swinging the flounce of her
dress on the tip of her foot. And they went on chat-
tering about clothes, although their hearts were not in
it. The deadly boredom of this day was never-ending.
Disappointed, Maria Antonia had wrapped up her

treasures.

It was raining on Orcino. It had been raining for two days. And the wind was bringing more rain. Four small earthenware stoves filled with embers were unable to take the chill out of the huge, low-ceilinged room, its walls paneled and covered with fabric trimmed with Greek motifs. The long white curtains, fringed with embroidered braid, had been opened completely; but even so, the light was still fragile, kept back by the iron mesh that protected the windows and by the veil of rain which undulated on the uneven surface of the panes, distorting the faraway vista. In the soothing half-light of a field of heather, the landscape, divided by those panes into squares, displayed out-of-the-ordinary colors, interspersed with tombstones and hedges. At the foot of one of them huddled a blue-flecked pond, made tiny by perspective, where the rain sparkled. From it flowed a secondary light, scarcely visible below a horizon for which evening was lying in wait, so that with each gust of wind an azure ray glanced off the boles of the shrubbery bordering the Castello di Pietra. Behind the knolls and hollows of the marshes rose a tall, rotting cross, wound around with twinning plants.

The sky was filled with farewells; the swallows, grouped in chorales, were preparing to leave, yielding their place to the gulls from the Gulf of Follonica. There was an abnormally high number of them for the season, presaging storms at sea. Autumn was descending on Italy from one end to the other, but on this ligneous, barren Tuscan landscape, it was already taking on a wintry aspect.

For a long, long time the Tolomeis' estate had been called the Castello di Pietra. An end-of-the-world site, a small, mute, fortified town. Anyone traveling in this part of southern Tuscany who takes the wrong road when he comes to the junction with the old la Spina toll barrier, beyond the river Bruna, a few leagues upstream from the ancient Etruscan city of Vetulonia, finds himself in a desolate and grandiose area with out-croppings of silver-bearing lead. It was here that the grand dukes' foundries once prospered, after the Spanish monarchs had abandoned this land, where they used to send their convicts. The powerful Panocchieschi family, long since ruined, had sold the castle to Niccolo, who much enjoyed living there. Unlike most of his neighbors and acquaintances, who rushed back to Pisa at the first signs of the cold season, he, Niccolo, then became a country dweller again. The two convoys would sometimes meet, going opposite directions along the road, and call each other names:

"Look at those tenderfeet, afraid of the frost!"

"And you, you wild tomcats!"

"Bunch of frozen asses!"

"You out to catch blackbirds?"

"Stay-at-homes!"

"Make-believe shepherds!"

And other gibes, all in good humor.

No court etiquette, no school of decorum could have given a woman or child that secret elegance, that bitter serenity to which a stay at Orcino is conducive.

Pia felt she was living there in a state of convalescence or, rather, of hibernation.

For some minutes she had been watching the rain run down the window, comparing the vast panorama encompassed in the narrow surface of a pane with her own dream, enclosed in the facades of this god-forsaken castle. While Magia wore her eyes out over her embroidery frame, Chiarina read aloud, haltingly, as if at school, from the pages of an old book by one Agnolo Firenzuola, recently re-published for "ladies of quality" with the promising title, *Della perfetta bellezza d'una donna*. Precepts for statues, really, without a hint of frivolity; an inventory of solemn, abstract virtues. Shivering, Pia shrugged her shoulders: that was all right for the old days, not for today; she would ask Niccolo to put new books in the library. But where could he be this time? Out hunting? Or hunting for harlots? He'd almost gone into mourning for Sigismondo, a dog!

Di qua e di lá del borgo
Tutti figli di Niccolo

(Here and there and throughout the village, they're all sons of Niccolo!), the young peasant girls on the estate sang, laughingly. She knew it. She would never have imagined it a few years earlier, when they were married in the good old cathedral church in Sovana. For the first time they had dressed her like a grown-up, ceremoniously. And Niccolo had seemed to her so handsome! No one, at the time, had made any disobliging remark about what was, for Niccolo, a second marriage. He had given her so much confidence in herself. For it had taken her a long time to feel secure about using her beauty, to convince herself of it. Before Niccolo, her life had not existed except in the form of an illness that had made her distant and unstable. Long before her, all her friends had become experienced, calculating women, luring suitors, while she, Pia, had thought herself ugly; and truth to tell, it was other people's insistence, Niccolo's especially, much more than her mirror, that had led her to give up her silly self-torment. Since then, what pains she was at to continue pleasing others and herself, looking for compliments, the only thing which encouraged her not to let herself go. To feel reassured, she had to live amid constant "hurrahs!" At Orcino, therefore, she was wilting from boredom; she would so much rather have stayed in Pisa, or amused herself in Florence or Siena. She had to be roused from a sleepiness that pervaded her, the more so since it was her very nature. With a thankfulness that was doubtless mingled with anxiety, she welcomed those seeking her favors, happy that they had something to ask of her, she who felt herself made so much more for receiving than for giving. Even so, one must not ask too much of her. This Frenchman, for instance: though flattered by his compliments, she found him dangerous, a threat to her comfort. He would be demanding, he would cause difficulties.

With Niccolo, it was different. He suited her temperament, ardent but passive. Since her wedding night, that had been so surprising to her, she had acquired an irremediable taste for servitude that was strangely close to gratitude. She was more than obedient: she was fascinated. How could she have resisted him? She would have had to deploy more strength than her inertia was capable of. And why should she wear herself out? After all, wasn't it preferable to have security and comfort rather than be tossed about, pierced, crucified by heart-rending affairs? How good it was to be inhabited within oneself by a will foreign to one's own! What a pleasure to go for hours without thinking, safe in a harbor manned and defended by others! How many times had her husband, in triumphant intimacy, told her that a woman was not made to think but "to be under-neath. . ."

Yet there was no denying that this world of calm meant for Pia the end of the world. She was choking on peacefulness and sadness at the same time. She was waiting. At the center of her humiliation remained an obscure feeling of revolt, of faith in an originality known only to her and stupidly spoiled by sub-missiveness to a master—and what a master! She had the impression of living in a lonely tête-á-tête with an unfulfilled destiny. Niccolo's love no longer satisfied her. . . His licentious caresses always made her woman's body tingle in an animality that momentarily oblit-erated her consciousness. Niccolo had an unequalled way of revealing to her that pleasure was an avowal of relationship to animals or stars—but stars with animal heat. When she swooned under her husband's domina-tion, a hoarse contralto song rose to her lips and from it emanated such a desolate weariness that it was like the marriage of seashore and wind. She quickly came to: in Niccolo's spirit was something that formed an obstacle to the familiarity of their bodies. That love was a blind sky, an evil fire, a conflict under a hovering, infernal void; to that felicity as keen as death her heart now rose only to be broken. Clearly now—so late!—she saw that love without love, the one that was neither ardor nor the gift or the forgetfulness of self, more closely resembled a funeral rite than the delicious feast it betokened. Sharing a man's life—that did not mean anything. Who, for that matter, has ever shared anyone else's life? Was she getting older? Gradually, in any case, she tended to simulate a sensual delight, a pleasure she no longer felt. She knew it was illusory to make an offering of her body and she was beginning to wonder if her ingenuous fraud was still able to deceive what she dared not call her husband's credulity.

Such were Pia's inward, somewhat reluctant meditations. That foreigner had opened a window in her heart. Yes, was she getting older?

Chiarina was still droning through *Della perfetta bellezza.* Magia was embroidering irises on the starched cloth and Pia, at the thought that she might be aging, began to massage her eyelids. At any rate she was a free creature no longer; nor would she ever be. The first question she had asked Niccolo during their brief betrothal period had been: "So, are you going to take charge of me?" Yes, she needed to be taken charge of. She had nothing to give; less than ever, now.

Changing her way of life, defying the law, setting out again in search of that invisible thing called hope: no, definitely not; her nonchalance was definitely not suited to that. A man has the possibility of being free; a woman, none. For a woman, freedom is synonymous with loneliness, the greatest of misfortunes. What did it matter that Niccolo was notoriously unfaithful, that she felt repugnance, that she made a calculated gift of her body swooning at the utmost extreme of pleasure? The fact was that she was married to a strong, clever man without whom, clumsy as she was at organizing her life, she would sink like a stone. With him, she would remain beautiful for a long time, safe from want; she would never be one of those old madwomen who collected cats or knitted for the soldiers. This hermetic palace, fortified like a prison, was also a reassurance, a refuge keeping her safe from others and herself. Then too, Niccolo had another quality, such an estimable one: he didn't need to have anyone love him; she wasn't yielding any of her soul to him; he didn't ask for it; on the contrary, souls frightened him. He demanded only that she be there, at his disposition for those "good hours," when he was in the body-desiring, "I-want-you" mood. So Pia could dispose of her soul as she liked, use it for dreaming, for witnessing from afar the delightful dramas that she made up or those that concerned other people, or again, the beginning of those very simple Eden-like friendships, saturated with purity, that were not compromising in any way.

She dreamed of that Frenchman she had met not long ago on the shores of the Atlantic, who loved her. What he had said to her warmed her, gave her a pious feeling. When would she see him again? Could it be that he would be willing to be the very pure and very simple friend, the gallant for whom her need for sincerity clamored today? Between Niccolo and him she would feel well balanced; her body belonged to the one, her loneliness to the other; she gave herself to the one, waited for the other. Her dissociated self could not see any way to salvation except in being attached to two men, since she despaired (at such a late date in her life: she was twenty-five already!) of being able to find one who would be hers, body and soul. If only this foreigner had appeared in the past at the door of the closed garden, on the threshold of the Villa Carlotta, her parents' home—she called it the House of Spirits—on

54

only their own image back to the three women. The castle was encircled by nothingness.

"What a pleasure it is to be bored, Chiarina. You put too much perfume on me. I smell like a whore."

"Will you be quiet! A fine thing indeed, to say such ugly words, and what is more, they are lies."

"Tell me, do you know the story of Kristine, Niccolo's first wife? No one has ever wanted to tell me about it."

"It is much better so. Keep your distance from gossip. Here, they lose no time in destroying a reputation."

"Whose reputation? I'm not a child, I want to know. Everything is kept from me."

"To tell you the truth, I don't know exactly what happened. She died far from here, shortly before your marriage. They buried her secretly. But why don't you ask Magia, since you're so curious? You were here before me, weren't you, Magia? And you knew the German woman, isn't that right?"

Magia was a cautious old woman who must have been given instructions, for she pretended not to hear.

"Magia, be nice, otherwise I will be thinking horrible things, and I'll be afraid."

"You will be much more afraid if I tell you, Signora."

"My dear, darling sweet little Magia, can you refuse me something—refuse it to me, Pia, who loves you? Remember what you asked me yesterday? Well, I'll give it to you if you tell me everything."

"You will regret it. . ."

"What do my regrets matter to you? I'm the one who gives the orders, Magia, don't forget. Tell me, my nice Magia. With lots and lots of description, to pass the time. Tell me. The men won't be back for a while yet."

Outside the chorales of swallows had fallen silent. Magia tightened her flounced cape about her, blew on her fingers wounded by the needle.

"Swear to me first that you will not repeat it; you will pretend that you know nothing. Swear it on the Three Nails. Do you know I've heard it said they buried her naked, the poor lady. . ."

"That's enough, Magia, stop. Pia won't be able to sleep tonight. Why doesn't she have her husband tell her the story?"

"Poor Kristine," mused Niccolo's wife out loud, "poor Kristine, she must have felt so cold; why did they do that?"

"No one even knows where her tomb is. They say that her name was not even engraved on it, just the Tolomei family name: as if she had never existed."

"And what was she like. . .before?"

As if she feared there would not be enough light on the resuscitating face of the unknown woman, Pia drew a lamp closer to her chair.

"What was she like?" she repeated, more softly.

"Peculiar; so peculiar that when she drove through Pisa in her open calash, people stopped to look at her. On Sundays, when the bridges were so crowded, when you saw all those people standing still to stare at her, it was as if the earth had stopped turning. And she was so tall, very tall; hard to think there had been room for her in her mother's womb. Kristine Daae, her name was, Kristine Daae."

"As tall as Niccolo?"

"Nearly; taller, even, when she wore heels. She had long blonde hair and wore it loose, on her shoulders. But her face was often inscrutable, her thin nose like a dagger, her eyes too blue. She also had a mania for wearing a chain with a single jewel around her forehead, which is not the custom with our women. And those breasts, placed so high up! Just below her neck; they held her dress taut like a drapery on a statue. Unfortunately, although you would not have thought so to look at her, she had inherited a frail constitution from her mother; she was constantly catching colds. Now what Niccolo needed was a woman who was a woman, by the Madonna! full of blood, full of life. Her wrist-bones were so big that she wore only open bracelets. Winter made her sad, the springtime irritated her, the summertime covered her with perspiration. Personally, I felt sorry for her. Toward the end she stopped wearing make-up. You'd have thought she had already stopped living.

"It is true that before the period I am talking about, there had been another period, a time when Niccolo and Kristine had loved each other very much. She went out and had fun and gave receptions, as much as you do now. But as I told you, she was from the north, too nostalgic for Niccolo. The open air here at Orcino and the way her husband neglected her drew her far away, into dream after dream, until she came to wish for less violent embraces than Niccolo's, if you will allow me, Madam. She conceived a passion for a young neighbor. They saw each other seldom, they say, and that was enough to give Kristine transports of joy. It was obvious there was something unheard of in the expression on her face. And this went on as long as he did not guess. . ."

"Because he guessed?"

"Worse than that: he saw. You know the grand stair-case. At the top, at that time, there was a brand new mirror; one of the few pieces of new furniture at Orcino. It was perhaps three o'clock that day, a lovely afternoon. There were a dozen of them who'd been out riding on the heath and were now returning gaily. Niccolo came up the stairs first; Kristine followed, on that young man's arm. I was waiting on the landing and with my own eyes I saw her lean her head, because she was tired, no doubt, on the companion's shoulder and I saw him—I think he did it automatically—lovingly put a stray lock of her thin hair back in place. Niccolo must have seen them in the mirror, the horseman's arm now around Kristine's waist. Not one remark was made; not a word was said. But Niccolo's face changed, while I saw the features of an unthinking Kristine soften in beatific joy. She was to pay so dearly for that joy!"

"My God! How?"

"We poor women are the playthings of lordly Man. Men are free to pursue birds of any kind of feather, we are locked in a cage; little matter whether its bars be of wood or gold. A woman, in our Italy, is a bird without wings, a hen mated to a hawk. If he hears an ant marching toward his captive, he waxes wroth and gobbles it up; woe to the spouse who so much as lets her eyes turn toward a passerby: they are gouged out for her. But Oneself—one runs, one gallops, one sniffs all the necklines, one mounts, one burns as soon as one is fanned by a skirt, one plays at 'take me as I am.' We women are supposed to grow hot only on command, while the men sizzle if you so much as graze them. Regular Judases!"

"That's a fine situation you're describing to us. But then what happened? Tell me what happened afterward."

"The very next day, without any ceremony, without so much as a farewell, she left Orcino before we were awake. It was Isidoro who drove her, in the cariole. Niccolo told us she had gone away to look after her health and that she would stay away a long time, a very long time. After that, I don't know any more."

"Yes, you do. Tell me some more. Come closer, right here by me."

"All that happened was that she died. There. That's all. They went to get her in the gilded, silk-upholstered carriage, the one that is used for weddings. There were only a few of us present at her burial. Her younger sister was there, and do you know something: she looked like you. Niccolo was attracted by her, and if she hadn't gone home to her own country immediately, who knows what might have happened? He was already beginning to court her. Every misfortune brings some good—and you have that resemblance to thank for the fact that you, dear Pia, are our mistress today."

"You haven't answered my question, Magia. You said she left Orcino—but where did she go? For how long?"

"Difficult to get that straight. Nowadays no one sets foot any more in an old shepherd's cottage on the Castagnola lands, down by Follonica. The sloughs all around it are swarming with mosquitoes that would eat you up alive, right up to your hair; the air is black and frozen, with great holes. What with the humidity, the fevers finish you off in a few days. You're walking along, you sink into a mud-hole, and all you can hear are the dismal birds hanging from the clouds. Malaria country. That is where Niccolo had her shut up, at least the way I've heard it. Isidoro was responsible for bringing her wood and food. A small drawing room had been arranged for her. And that is where she lived for years, the life of a bat, of an excommunicated woman with neither priest nor prayers. Niccolo never spoke of her again. Neither did we, and we didn't see her again until her burial—and even that is just a figure of speech, for Isidoro had already nailed down the coffin. She was an abandoned creature. Who is to say whether she didn't die of starvation? As for the pretty young man she had loved, let me tell you: he continued coming to the house, a dandy with his boots and his cane, his slick hair and his wandering hands, never saying a word about her, never shedding a tear or even sighing a sigh. Ah, men! *Miserere nobis, Domine.* And that is the whole story. At least she died married, a proper wife, with her ring on her finger. Then you came along, radiant, holding hands with Niccolo; the ring you are wearing. . ."

"No, this one is mine. My mother gave it to me. You are wicked, Magia."

"I love you, Pia; my only wish is that you should not cease to be happy. There must not be any ghosts to bother you. Not only did Kristine die but she also, believe me, went back to her city on the Rhine, afterwards."

"What is this gypsy story you're telling me, Magia? You would have me believe that the dead go traveling!"

"But just listen while I explain it to you. In the afternoon, when the burial was over, we were here in the courtyard; the air was hot. Kristine's sister was talking to Niccolo, while the two greyhounds, Sigismondo and Moro, lay at their feet. You know how fond Niccolo was of Sigismondo, claiming he could scent things from beyond the grave, that he was far more intelligent than people were. It was so pleasant in the courtyard that no one was thinking of the deceased. You cannot imagine how fine the weather could be at Orcino in those days. Now the seasons are old and more or less chilled through but in the past, how fine the weather used to be! Everywhere—outdoors, indoors, in the trees, in our hearts! Isidoro had gone to get a whip, and the carriage was just waiting for him before taking Kristine's sister away; she was preparing to say goodbye. It was the horses who began: they stared off toward Follonica in such an absorbed way that Sigismondo pointed his muzzle stubbornly in that direction. Then Moro woke up. At that point Isidoro came back but no one paid any attention to him; we were all turned toward Follonica: in a sort of panting of the sea-wind, we felt, coming toward us, the presence of a person who had breathed. And suddenly the horses whinnied. Sigismondo, bewitched by that neighing, got up and majestically, like someone who is acquainted with the customs, he walked forward, as if he knew exactly whom he was walking to. He stood up very tall, laid his head in a lap of air, and yelped; then, intrigued, he fell back with a lugubrious howl that made us shudder. A bird that had been in the pear tree all of a sudden flew away. The most affected of us all was Niccolo. His eyes searched the sky—searching for what? Then he shrugged his shoulders as if to say that he couldn't do anything about it. He called back the dog, but Sigismondo did not obey him; on the contrary he continued to caper about and mark sudden, plaintive pauses. The horses shivered all down their veined necks. We would all have gone on standing there and waiting if Niccolo hadn't reached out his hand, not without brutality, and furiously opened the door of the calash to seat his sister-in-law in it; the whip cracked; but oddly enough, before the horses got under way, the door opened by itself, then closed, while the springs sagged as if a second person had just climbed in. Although the two hounds had been trained never to run after carriages, they ran after this one for a very long time. And exceptionally, their master did not scold them. Some days later he had the mirror at the top of the staircase removed; it no longer had any reason to be there, he said, 'since it was empty.' "

"Oh, but I see! What you're telling us is the story of Parisana."

"Parisana?"

"Yes, a film that was shown in Grosseto last year. The daughter of squire Pesaro, one Andrea Malatesta, married the very wicked Marquis d'Este, who had already spawned nearly a dozen bastards. She was young, she was very beautiful, her name was Parisana. It was Ugo, one of her husband's illegitimate sons, who courted her. One day the duke caught sight of them, embracing, in a mirror. My God, it still makes me tremble, he had both of them put on trial. I can still see them, sitting side by side in a very high-ceilinged room; next to them had been placed cups for them to drink out of, little cups such as I have never seen.

From time to time a bailiff came to light their faces with his candlestick to see if they were ashamed; but no, they were not ashamed; nor were they in a hurry; a mere nothing was enough to divert them: through the open window, they watched a valet cutting the gorse bushes in the dark moat about the castle of Ferrara. The scythe whistled sharply. They were both beheaded below the Tower of the Lions; as they crossed the courtyard they raised their eyes to the May night and then she said something to him sweetly, I don't remember what. It's strange but it seemed to me her voice was familiar."

Pia did not stop looking at the darkness through the pouring rain. All these stories they were telling her seemed drowned by it; also, she wished to affect, before her women attendants, an indifference which would shield her from their curiosity. Besides, her emotion was mingled with sweetness: the death of the two lovers fulfilled her dreams more than it aroused fears; the moats of Ferrara seemed to her the most voluptuously propitious of beds for the ultimate embrace. And she meanwhile, prisoner of this gray stone castle, was wearing herself out with acquiescing in a matrimonial fate as slow and sluggish as mud. Oh, if only those who would hasten the speed of time would come! Oh, if he would come who would harness the incredible, inexhaustible quantity of strength placed at her heart's disposal. Ah but no, no after all, she did not feel herself capable of so dangerous a destiny. Woman she was, and woman she remained, even so far as to take pleasure in a melancholy that came to her from being inhabited by several worlds at once in a state of terror that bruised and exalted her at the same time. It is certain that nature had designated her to feel things without authorizing her to clarify them one bit, in order, no doubt, that she remain the unconscious and ravished expression of their secret. . .

5

To Castagnola, the little promontory above the cove at Follonica, no one came but Sunday fishermen. It had long since lost its inhabitants and the architectural decors it had possessed in the days of the grand dukes. All that remained of them, and that cropped up out of a mangy lawn, were pieces of a mosaic, and a yellow brick partition on which a fresco painting stood out, the anemic profile of what had been a cross-bowman. Where the waters of a pool had splashed there now leaped only the forequarters of a stone horse, surprised at seeking the reflection of his nostrils without breath in the invisible water. Disorderly trees which the lightning had stripped of their marrow squeezed the seascape in their embalmers' fingers: they were resin pines, colder than colonnades, rutted by rills of rain. They rose out of foothills that were too rounded to be natural, too

69

symmetrical, perpetually chilled by a wind that made them bristle with the splinters of low-lying vegetation.

This particular morning, the rains had moved farther off. A dazzling light swept into the village, reduced to a parallelogram surrounded, except on the side toward the sea, by one-story houses, all of them closed. Pia was coming by the cliff path. All along the interminable shore where the autumn was growing she kept coming, riding Rosso, the handsome trotter, while the dead leaves fled in hordes and the wind spoke to her of Kristine Daae, of that story she had not yet dared mention to Niccolo. But just what exactly was she coming to look for in Castagnola? Now that everything had disappeared, now that the wind passed through the trees, the sea and the walls as easily as through a net, what did she hope to gain by a visit to Castagnola? How could she reconstitute things which had never existed in her memory and which she glimpsed only through others' memories? Really, what was she coming to find or conjure up in Castagnola? Kristine resuscitated, standing on her doorstep of grass? An excuse for her nascent love for the Frenchman? The exact notes of a disturbing melody which must have been filling the air of Pisa and Orcino for a long time without her knowing it and which she had just begun to heed? How insinuating it was, in any case, this wind that was telling her the story of Kristine Daae! And how closely the landscape was watching her! You would think they had arranged this trip to Castagnola between them. Over there, on the right hand, always the same sodden island, with its cliff that gave off an odor of alabaster, its scorched ferns and its sheep in the summer. Over there, to the left, the discontinuous colors of the village walls. Nothing had changed. The climate had not grown any gentler around the last home of Kristine Daae. The weather here stood by its hostility. Several years afterward it continued to signify the same thing. And it was this orderly continuity of time, space and things which established between Orcino and Castagnola, between Pia and Kristine, as much as between the Frenchman, Niccolo and Kristine's suitor, a fateful relationship.

As she penetrated into this unwonted landscape, where everything should have frightened her, compared with the sumptuousness of Pisa or the etiquette of Orcino, Pia, on the contrary, did not feel herself in the least out of place, so haunted was this site by her own drama. No matter where one goes, one does not alter one's fate. She clearly saw that here on earth, notwithstanding the exterior things which seem to transform themselves, there is the eternal decor, within us and before you, oh my God, of a fate we act out without being masters of our role, spectators that we are of a life that is imposed on us. All we need do is scratch the varnish of the faces we see about us—and we discover other faces, faces from the past, traced over each other by passing time. Under her own features, Pia felt Kristine's face quiver; through her own love showed the love of the unhappy woman exiled at Castagnola.

One imagines one is original and inimitable; one imagines one is free, hoping that this freedom will make life intelligible and simple, when, on the contrary, it becomes deliberately more complicated until at last it merges with those ardent, unfortunate existences of which the past offers so many examples. Every time we start an adventure as our very own, life very quickly makes us understand that it refuses that pretention, since what we call initiative is merely the sequel to a story begun by others, long before we have become conscious of it. We confine ourselves to being the reflections of our predecessors. Unaware, we second fate. What we call time is a ceaseless reminder of the past.

To the rhythm of the horse's gait, now climbing toward the citadel from the deserted hamlet, Pia swam back up the stream of days to identify herself with Kristine. Was it not true that the same man had fashioned each of them according to his own desires? Didn't the same adulterous love, the same complicity beckon to them? Castagnola, with its mute and desolate streets, recalled the expanses that ringed the walls of Orcino—but also the glittering evenings in Pisa, whose gilt backdrop concealed a vast solitude of the soul. The air here was just as stifling. Through the magic of this autumn day, another woman's past was becoming Pia's present.

Having come to a dressed stone pavement onto which opened a narrow glazed door, Pia jumped down from her horse. She stepped over the threshold of what seemed to her a demolished garden, came to a second threshold, that of the house, leaned close to the glistening pane and found that it did not bring light onto the wall of a room but rather, onto a very high horizon where gulls were floating. Their flight as well as the azure spaces circumscribed by their cries were reflected, in turn, in a pair of mirrors which Pia's oblique gaze discovered a little way to the left, at the back of an alcove which had kept most of its walls.

"My God, where am I? What happened here?" she whispered, then pushed open the door and found herself in the remains of a drawing room almost empty of furniture. The light, entering the room with the straggling wind, became disturbing. For a shepherd's cottage, it was relatively luxurious. To left and right, under two small Napoleonic crests, two other chambers opened out, no bigger than the drawing room and with roofs that were almost intact. Their walls were covered with sateen held in place by strips of black wood. In the corner, a crystal cabinet held a statuette of a horseman wearing a checkered cloak. In addition to mirrors set with pearls, pieces of glass and precious stones, there were remarkable green drapes, a green carpeting, two trunks; in one of these, whose lid was open, was a jumble of laces and ribbons, ornamental mats embroidered like banners, skeins of thread, a jacket collar with octagonal buttons. On the convex lid of the other trunk lay a pair of open-work elbow-length gloves with rust-stained fingertips. The person who used to live here had obviously been interrupted in the midst of her occupations, only a few hours, or perhaps less, before her death. Shortly before her life ended, she had been concerned about her appearance: she had needed her gloves. She might have been smiling, for all about her she had things full of tenderness. And that, no one had told Pia. While she stood there, thinking about this, she noticed that the fireplace was full of half-burned logs, that all the lamps were clustered around the trunks, as if

74

the person had wanted to have as much light as possible
to help her with some painstaking task. So it must have
been night, and it must have been winter.

"Where are you?" she called. But the silence was
deaf. She was afraid.

Afraid that the disjointed roof would collapse on her;
afraid of this morning light which was more and more
intensely alive, awakening the soft shadow in the
mirrors, recoloring the drapes, touching the frames, the
paintings, the crowned women with bronze fingers,
bringing the ghosts alive. Outside, Pia's horse began to
whinny. Farther away, a second horse whinnied in
reply. "Where are you?" she repeated more loudly. In
echo came the sound of one horse, then of two, trot-
ting. Pia saw their two heads come close together,
remain immobile neck against neck; she recognized one
of the horses from the stables at Orcino. He was not
saddled. Now now, what was Pia imagining? Weren't the
horses around Orcino allowed to roam freely at certain
hours of the day? She stooped to button the jacket both
of whose arms were hanging to the floor; one button
came off, slid down the loose thread and rolled on the
mud-soiled carpeting; she pursued it with a feeling that
someone was fleeing before her; but she did not find it.
She went to one window, then another, then another;

the sun was now making the bushes blaze on the island of ferns and the horses were still whinnying. In the shadow she mistook a chest of drawers enveloped in a white slip-cover for a person, seated. She cried out in fright at sight of a plump dimpled hand laid on a sofa, palm up: it was a plaster hand, the kind antique dealers have to sell, reminiscent of the casts made of the hands of celebrated pianists when they die. After her cry, the house kept quiet while at the same time it filled with light, as the day advanced.

This daylight which came bursting into the Castagnola autumn had something springlike about it. A spring that was singularly more vivid than all that survived here, more vivid than herself, no doubt, difficult to understand. It gave the furniture, the shapes of things, the countryside the appearance that they must really have had when there was no one there to look at them or talk about them. It was this daylight which now, on the contrary, had begun to look at Pia, directing questions at her face, dressing her person in the outline of Kristine Daae. Unexpectedly, it had just inverted the roles without her realizing it, placing her in its power, making her submit.

The effect of this inquisition by the reinvigorating springtime light was to make Pia feel herself become very beautiful—and very faint; her presence yielded to another presence, incommensurable, inexpressibly captivating, cancelling her soul, turning her into a consenting animal. Oh, to run away, to give herself up to any creature stirred by the same dream, to become a mere river of blood! She looked for her horse so as to huddle against him, warm herself and find herself against him, kiss his neck and his quivering nostrils, rid herself of the frightening solitude she felt because this light was making her an object of desire! The two horses, rearing chest to chest, with their eyes rolled back and their hooves striking together, playfully bit each other's manes; their strength seemed to lift up the entire landscape, and their whinnying was so frequently underscored by plaintive cries that it would have been impossible to say whether this was the echo of the waves biting the cliff or that of the gulls aiming to climb up to the few clouds that floated above the colonnade of pines.

"How beautiful I feel!" she said out loud, adding, "beautiful and useless". . .and her eyelids half-closed on a melancholy pride.

Placing her hands on her hips, she walked, provocatively, toward one of the spotted, rust-speckled mirrors; one of those spots, the size of a handkerchief, deprived her of the reflection of her head. So it was she saw her own decapitated body coming to meet her in this glass where the greenness of the sea, the greenness of the headlands, the greenness of the sky formed a garden.

"It's as if there was nobody there," she thought, trying in vain to find herself a face between the blots on the mirror, all the while stroking her silken hips.

"Where am I?"

The echo of the sea, the woods of Castagnola rising like a forest of masts sent back to her the image of that street by the Atlantic where last year she had met, for the first time, a stranger to whom she had not been introduced. But wait, come to think of it, how did the words of the *Canzoniere* go? *"Il 6 Aprile 1327 nella chiesa di Santa Chiara, la bellezza e la grazia di una gentildonna accesero in lui un amore che non si estinse mai più." Mai più. . .* (. . .lighted within him a fire of love which never more went out.). May his love remain to me, as in the book. . .

"Oh that awakening inside of me, when he spoke to me. And that caress and those lips. . . You are the one through whom things become beautiful. Thanks to you I have seen the unforgettable. We live on the same dream but I inhale yours more avidly than you do, since your dream is me. There by the Atlantic, how happy I

the master hired me. I smoke out moles, I burn cater-
pillars, I flay foxes. And by the Holy Trinity, Signora, a
fox is as sly as Calabrian wine; a regular ruffian and
cocky as the devil, believe me; you've got to be clever if
you don't want to fall for the way that hypocritical
good-for-nothing says his prayers; but by the pope!
there's not one of them that's fallen into my hands but
what I've scrubbed his tonsure for him, I can tell you!
The one I'm talking about had done so much thieving
that, by the Holy Shroud, he was brought under the
mulberry tree to be skinned alive; I'd already slit the
skin off that trollop's neck when what does she do but
escape; yes, it was a she-fox; away she did run with that
piece of skin wrapped around her like a nightgown—and
where was she running, do you think? Right to her den,
where those insolent little cubs of hers were waiting for
her. I picked up the whole litter and to teach them a
lesson, I had them watch while their mother sweated it
out. Trashy beasts! And tough they are too, you know;
she died without crying, biting the stick we'd put
between her jaws. Rest assured, Signora, I destroy only
what is harmful."

"Do you remember? Did you see her? Tell me."

"Who are you talking about, Signora?"

"She died without crying, did you say?"

"She did that, the vixen. . ."

"Is this where it happened?"

"Here? No, over there, under the mulberry tree, as always, where we hang up the meat before cutting it into pieces, as Signora well knows."

"And she wasn't afraid?"

"Yes, she shivered as if she was cold, and yet she was dancing about as if she was possessed."

"The lamps were lighted, the logs were burning; she spoke to you. . ."

"That trollop? She yelped and winced all at the same time, you mean, and her blood burned my fingers."

"Poor, poor friend. . .Did she live in this house a long time?"

"To the very end."

"And it was you who took care of the house, wasn't it?"

"Yes, she liked me; the sadder she was, the prouder she got."

"And then what?"

"And then one day toward the end of winter, in the little drawing room, she left us; it happened very quickly; I found her on the sofa, as sure as I'm seeing you; she was like this, look."

"They say she had stopped eating. . ."

"They may say what they want to; that's her fault, not mine. Nobody could help it. From biting her lips with remorse all the time she'd become so thin it was frightening, but she kept quiet. She used her fist like a stone to strike her stomach. When I begged her to eat, she would make a sign to me: "Later," she was saying, "later." If I tried to insist, she would look at me silently, in such a tired way. It's a miracle she lasted so long."

"When you found her on the sofa, it was a few days before Easter, wasn't it?"

"Ah! so Signora knows? How is that?"

Her betrothal period—Pia relived it now: interminably long, each day Niccolo more exasperated with impatience, anxious to hasten the wedding. One afternoon, when he was about to take leave of her, he had suddenly turned around and walked toward her with his hands behind his back as if hiding a surprise, telling her with almost alarming determination, "Tomorrow, we'll put an end to this." She had answered, half teasing, half solemn, that they would see about that; she was not at all surprised that nothing happened the next day, nor the next, nor the days that followed. Nothing until that very week before Easter, when she noticed that Niccolo seemed transformed, that he was commencing to reconsider everything from the beginning, having at last put a certain distance between himself and something or someone. There could be no doubt about it. By a silent agreement, she had refrained from asking him why he wore the triumphant expression that comes from having at last accomplished a long-deferred duty. She herself was so avid for the felicity of marriage that she paid no attention to what preceded it, giving herself over body and soul to the expectation of what would follow it. Only later, through feigned inadvertence, she had learned that Niccolo had already been married to a foreign woman whose insignificance seemed obvious to her, compared to her own beauty. Therefore she did not recall having been the least bit jealous: just imagine, such an unreasonably unworthy feeling! And then too, hadn't the most necessary thing been achieved? Had she not, through marriage, been enclosed in a tranquil geometry which made the real and the marvelous converge in its lines, establishing supreme repose in the space surrounding it? But now, into that state of calm, in among the coombs of the sea, fears penetrated; one of them had the pupil of Isidoro's eyes, another the bared veins of the raging she-fox, another Kristine's gown with its disrupted folds and her long rust-stained glove; the last fear being a shapely hand which placed a golden wedding band on her own, while organ music breathed above her head. Hardly had that ring imprisoned her than she felt herself drifting into solitude, out of the innocent world of her family certainties, slipping into shapes and colors that were suddenly problematical; here came an animal bristling with fever, half-flayed, staggering as it fled through thorn hedges as far as the eye could see; above them spasmodically surged a long, pale, cadaverous, Rhenish face which, with its hair held back by a patterned band, contemplated its reflection in a mirror where—it was Pia who appeared.

Ricorditi di me che son la Pia.
Siena mi fé; disfecemi Maremma;
Salsi colui che inanellata pria
Dispando m'avea con sua gemma.[1]

Dante's poetry spoke with a voice which was her own; she lived those verses like an inward commemoration. Fulfilling her destiny amounted to following a path which had been laid out long since and followed by

---

[1] Remember me, who am La Pia;
Siena made me, Maremma unmade me;
He knows it who, wedding me,
Placed his gem upon my finger.

Dante, *Purgatory,* Canto V

other women of whom she was the unconscious heiress and, even more, the accurate image.

"And now, the house, without Kristine: what is to become of it?"

"Oh, the master has thought of that; he has ordered a mason and a carpenter to make it pretty, as it was before. He says it might come in handy again."

So then, in this setting suited to somber events, the past had caught up with them—she the haughty wife of Niccolo dei Tolomei, he the sordid valet, for whom any task was acceptable. And since it was the time of year when the equilibrium of nature is such that the social hierarchy is altered by it, they rode back to Orcino side by side, swiftly. The hills in front of the horses dropped like drawbridges. Above Kristine's small farm, the wind was gathering together the last birds. Pia was afraid of Isidoro because he was not a creature of God; she was afraid of Castagnola because it was a merciless land, deliberately chosen to cause suffering: under this sky of light and delight, what a place for a Calvary! But she promised herself none the less to return to Castagnola very soon, for there she had just discovered her own most profound, most inexplicable being; within her, Castagnola had created a new space in which the lines determining her existence were engraved, as in the palm of her hand. And it was here that she wanted to meet that foreigner, the Frenchman—for the sake of both tempting and warding off the devil.

Though bitten with cold, the air was superb above the estate, among the taciturn hills where the copses cast rounded, triangular shadows. Pia avoided Isidoro's gaze, masked with deference but perfectly dry, neither limpid nor gleaming, never answering queries; the gaze typical of those murderous bodyguards one sees in the works of Lombard painters: wrapped in scaly armour, like old lizards, they force themselves, condescendingly, to raise their heavy metal eyelids. Isidoro, having too much to say, said nothing. The two horses, their hooves buried in the whirling, rustling leaves, seemed to be wading in a crimson river. The mane on the forehead of Isidoro's horse was elegantly combed; he was showing off, pricking up his ears with a mannered and altogether Siennese jauntiness, doubtless imagining that he was being ridden by the Holy Sacrament.

"*Un' sbirro spavaldo* (an impudent servant)," she thought to herself.

"She's in danger, the conceited female," he said to himself.

Later, when she looked back on this day, she was to discover that it was then that she had accidentally struck a chord she should not have struck, for its vibrations had ripped her apart inside, incurably. She had moved without transition from a warm and naïve world into another, glacial and cunning, peopled by human beasts; more experienced than the wolf of Gubbio that dissolved in tears before the Poverello, they were steeped in implacable hatreds.

For the moment, galloping through these pastoral regions where only the animals could consider themselves really happy, Pia was hastening toward Orcino, her prison, a village without streets where the pigs and the dogs wandered, untended and unchecked. Solitary and enclosed in its walls, like a Vatican, the Castello di Pietra could be seen in the midst of its mirroring pools, darting its sharp lighting rods like rapiers into the fantastic radiance of its faded horizons.

The instant she dismounted, she felt that something was wrong. She would have liked to hide her face from these servants, who were looking at her as if they knew what she did not dare know herself. Those who did not look at her but, on the contrary, passed by her with a carelessness that was both pitying and ostentatious, embarrassed her even more; they went back and forth in the courtyard, carrying sacks of chestnuts gathered that morning, bending under their burden as under the

88

weight of a secret sadness of which she was doubtless the object.

The season would be growing colder and colder. Soon the fruit would have been picked, the animals shut in. The festivities in the drawing rooms of Pisa would gleam in her memory with a ruddy glow until winter ended. Soon the worst would come: the Frenchman's departure, loneliness, fear and then, back there in Castagnola, a dead house that Niccolo wanted to restore and refurnish—for what reason? For whom?

This thought did not deter her from admiring herself in the mirror of her bedchamber, where Chiarina was now undressing her, while she tried the effect of a pearl at her ear.

"I have not seen my husband, Chiarina; did he give orders for this evening?"

In reply, Chiarina handed Pia a note from Niccolo. Accustomed to the busy life of a spouse whose way of spending his time she knew virtually nothing about, she was astonished at his announcing to her that he was leaving unexpectedly for Pisa on urgent business. He would be back in two days at the most. She should enjoy herself in the open air and not catch cold. . .

And suddenly Pia took her decision.

"You too, Chiarina, will leave for Pisa tomorrow;

arrange it with Isidoro, it's his day off, I believe. . ."

"Of course, but what would I go to Pisa for?"

"You can help me. Do not laugh, this is serious. You'll go to Pisa, unless you're afraid of the rain, Chiarina, my little frog, my little witch. But careful you don't run away. Do you know the Nettuno?"

"Why do you ask me? And how sad you are!" Chiarina went on, in a lower voice, as she noticed a shade of reticence on her mistress's face. She felt Pia taking first one of her hands, then the other; she did not squeeze them but just held them together, fearfully, in her own hands:

"You are twenty, Chiarina, but you are an angel. You are not any age at all, like the angels. You are my joyous little sister; what could I tell you that you have not already understood? You will take to Pisa the letter I will give you."

"Take it to whom?"

It was her mistress's silence which gave Chiarina the full answer.

"What if he is already gone?"

But Pia was not listening to her any more; seated at her writing desk, she had begun to write her letter to the Frenchman. At dawn the next day, Chiarina, filled with presentiment, took advantage of the carriage to go into town; and Isidoro, seeing Pia wave to her maidservant from the window, smiled and smiled.

6

What with those inordinately high ceilings, which made heating it impossible, the Hotel Nettuno, at number 7, Lungarno Reggio, lost in the autumn the charm which its view of the bridges and the river conferred on it during good weather. The last travelers packed their bags. Although the climate of Pisa was generally mild in winter, it was humid and incompatible, warned the travel agencies, with rheumatism and gout.

"Ahi! Pisa vituperio della gente," murmured the hotel doorman, "accursed Pisa, proud Pisa, our Italy's city of glory and death. You see now, sir, Pisa is a city from which Christ has disappeared. Don't be taken in by our churches, by the marvelous existence of our pretty girls; it's not because Saint Peter stopped at our town first, at San Pietro in Grado, that crime and the devil do not prowl along our little streets; the women are more

92

shameless than they are elsewhere—think of the *Vergognosa di Pisa,* in our Camposanto Ubaldo, who looks on so avidly at Noah's drunkenness. And now that summer has gone you'll see how death is going to take advantage of that, to grow bigger; the Duomo, the baptistry and the campanile will be whiter and colder than ever; as for the Camposanto, which is crawling with buried souls, it's not just the dead people of Italy that turn over and over in it, but also the black faces from over the sea that were buried here pellmell, along with the fifty vessels of earth brought from the Mount Calvary: vagabonds, infidels, whatever you want to call them—*campo dell' infernale sonno!* You are right to go away, sir; if I could, I too would go away with you. Everyone says it is so nice in France! *Ahi! Pisa, vituperio della gente!*

"Such strong language, dear Andria! And such despair!"

"In the Italy of today, sir, hope is a miracle, and I have not experienced a miracle. Also, I cannot stand the Tuscans."

"I thought you came from here."

"Me, a Tuscan? You cannot mean that, sir, surely. Know that I am a Sardinian, from Villacidro. Ah, the great groves of orangetrees on the windblown esplanades of Villacidro! Honest folks they are in Villacidro, with high-bred hearts, not libertines, demoniacs, murderers like these Tuscans with their pointed knees; a grab-bag of tricks, the Tuscans are. When they go away you'd think they were coming toward you; when they laugh you'd think they were sneezing; they don't even pray on their knees, the way we do, but standing up, as if they were telling the Lord, 'you won't get me.' And when they assassinate you, they're the ones who cry for help. They receive you as sumptuously as a pope, but watch out—they're doing it to make you trust them so that they can fleece you and conceal their rapacity that much better. After you shake hands with one of them, best count your fingers; it would be surprising if there weren't some missing. Unbelievers too, on top of it all, waiting till the bells have chimed the signal for the Hail Mary—to bite their mistress's lips. *Maledetti!*"

"And so I'm going to say goodbye to them, Andria. I go back to France tomorrow. I meant to stay here for only a few days, anyway, just time enough to visit some friends; I don't know whether they are worse than the others but I love them even though I don't always understand them."

"If I were you, sir, I would keep a respectful distance from them. . ."

94

"They are artists, Andria, great artists; one must forgive them. . ."

"Artists they may be, but confirmed liars too. Even their precious Dante is a liar. In the Piazza dei Cavalieri—all the tourists are told this story—used to stand the Torre dei Gualandi alle sette Vie, where the accursed archbishop Ruggieri degli Ubaldini had Ugolino starve to death with his sons and his nephews. You know the story. But why did Alighieri put Ugolino in Inferno? He had merely defended his country against the Genovese; it was the archbishop who was a traitor, not Ugolino. But these Tuscans are all the same; they're a cruel and unjust race. You cannot imagine the number of unfortunate men and women that have been got rid of in this city's jails or on the farms in the maremma, by letting malaria eat them up or by just forgetting them, without even bread and water; and why, I ask you? On the strength of what? On the strength of a mere suspicion; a mere glance at another man, and a woman deserves death. The women here are a bold lot, no doubt about it, but their husbands are a bunch of rascals; they spy on them from morning till night and hire myrmidons to take note of every movement they make. Not that they are madly in love with their wives but because any unfaithfulness would be an outrage to what they care about most on earth: their arrogance. In Tuscany, a cuckold forfeits his place in the noisy circle of men, and he cannot bear that. On Sundays, after mass, in the church square, when he is about to start crowing like the others, 'And I did this, and I did that. . .,' he sees his neighbor's eye light up; he knows his neighbor is going to answer. 'Yes, and your wife did this, and your wife did that.' How could any Pisan stand for that? Better to die; no, better to kill. That's the way the Pisan are. But they'll all end up in Inferno themselves with their victims' teeth stuck in their skulls, by way of crowns. Leave this country, sir, and let them bathe in the sulphur of their sins.''

Andria was wasting his time, for the Frenchman was already filled with regret. Let Andria express himself so harshly; after all, he was pursuing a quarrel between Italians. But over him, the man come from the Atlantic, Pisa cast an invincible spell. No matter that the swallows were darting their already frosted wings through the air; their cries continued to cheer him. Suppose this was springtime, he thought. Would the weather be any clearer, the flowers more abundant? In France, certainly not; the seasons die more quickly there and people stay at home; whereas the streets of Pisa were still alive with strollers whom the autumn, here and there, touched with colors that made them resemble those painted crowds in the frescoes you see in apses, between the Turkish trophies and the galleys of the battle of Lepanto. Several beautiful faces, beseechingly shy, were a reminder that Pisa, though a poor city, was also a cordial universe. *"Fiori, cartoline e belle cose"* read the sign above one shabby shop, squeezed in between two sumptous town houses. *"Core ornato di fiori e di frutti"* proclaimed an alluring theater bill. And each tree resounded differently amid its leaves; each district gave off its own odor: here a grassy exhalation, there an intoxication of garden between two warm walls, farther on a wafting scent of woodwork mixed with oil paint. Men, buildings and things literally feasted and made merry in Pisa, but their fancifulness was contained within the medieval ordonnance of the military archi-tecture. Like churches designed to bring together throngs of pilgrims with their crowds of children and enjoin them to silence through the impressive dimen-sions of their vaulted ceilings, so the monuments of Pisa keep the multitudes orderly. The anarchical poor taste of the Ligurian riviera has never yet succeeded in pene-trating inside the walls of Pisa. Andria was right: the Pisans' exorbitant pride must stem from their certainty that the world was subservient to them, since it had so

97

docilely obeyed their geometers. In any case, the beauty of this autumn was so perfect that it had certainly never had its equal at any time, not even in the days of Diotisalvi, of Pisano or Byron; not even during the so-called happy years of the reign of Victor Emmanuel II. For it was Pia's autumn, and there would never be another to demonstrate like this one the enchantment of a man conquered by the country of a woman loved.

"You are mistaken, Andria. Allow me to tell you that I will be heavy-hearted on leaving Pisa, that I will continue to feel very grateful to you and that one day, perhaps, I will come back. Even if only to enjoy the organ of San Stefano's once more."

For surely no one can remain insensitive to the accents of the organ of San Stefano's during high mass. There you are, contemplating the colonnades, straining to hear the words of the mass when, suddenly, a music appears which, coming through space, immediately alters the lines, the substance and the spirit of space. It awakens the trees, although they are already shivering on their feet as they reach into the church; it seeks out the sturdy souls of the animals that spill joyously into the nave as if from Noah's Ark; it deluges the insolent heads, so that they are suddenly stamped with the seal of fish, of cetaceans, of sea- or river-monsters, surprised at feeling integrated into a botanical and zoological universe from which they had haughtily considered themselves distinct. Every man who hears the organ of San Stefano's forgets that he is a man; your nearest neighbor becomes a donkey, the second on your right begins to moo, another turns around with an almost threatening air—he looks like a lion; others have become bushes, or harpsichords, or sparrows. The entire church, restored to the primitive swarming of the creatures, abruptly voided of any sin of intelligence, bursts into a paradisiacal celebration—through the magic of the organ of San Stefano's. (Why isn't this mentioned more often? There is no doubt that if we only knew it, nothing could prevent us from running more often to San Stefano's. Unless we didn't want to be one with the animals and the plants of the earth; such disdainfulness would be a pity; it would deprive us of all understanding of pleasure, happiness, music. Truly, truly, whoever is not capable of turning into a donkey or an ox has no business being in San Stefano's, since he will not enter the kingdom of heaven.) And it is not only animated beings that one hears living and singing to the breathing of the organ in San Stefano's; there are also the stones that secretly strut; the deepest notes of the music find their harmony in the occult heart of the stones deliberately hewn in order to bring each limb of the edifice into balance; they represent the shadow from which they were extracted, the furze and gorse they may have carried, the sands which retained them. If you are not to be moved by this, your heart must be harder than rock. Those who seem to be led accidentally to San Stefano's on a Sunday are not long in guessing that there was nothing accidental about it, that unbeknownst to them someone had invited them there; otherwise it would be unbearable, even frightening. From the instant they have understood that this time, at last, they have taken their first step in God's territory, from that minute on they will never be alone again, and the expressions they will use in talking about Pisa, about what they remember, about the people they chanced to meet— they will see that those expressions come from the language of love. Little by little they will discover the name of the man or the woman by whom they were tacitly invited to go on the journey of love, even if that person is not there waiting for them when they arrive. Concerning the man or the woman who has thrust them into this incredible adventure, it is possible that they may not even be able to tell anything; first of all because everything happens so unexpectedly that they cannot find words for it, and then because no one would

100

believe their story. How could one seriously think of saying, "I had a rendez-vous with a woman I did not know; and at this rendez-vous there was no one, or next to no one; instead I saw a celebration. I heard an organ, I saw other guests who were there to stay, one way or another, without there being anything embarrassing nor unexpected, properly speaking, about her absence or their presence. A mystery? Why, there is nothing mysterious about it."

"Don't you see, Andria, I do not believe in Pisa's opprobrium nor in the Tuscans' curse. I personally will never be able to speak about Pisa except lovingly. Although. . ."

One weekday, when it was already growing dark, he had entered that very church of San Stefano's, attracted by muffled fragments of scales, and it was then he had begun to understand. The same authoritarian fingering had received him once before, conducting the funeral strains of the *Tuba mirum* through the drawing rooms on that anniversary evening. This must be Pia's husband. The music rose, utterly alone, neither the stones nor the creatures participating in it; assailed by its strains, the columns tottered, lost their foundations; all around, the earth seemed to dissolve, crash down, then evaporate in a nebulous transposition; the vigor of the marble, the joints of the flooring, the solidity of bodies—all of this melted into that music which destroyed substance and left only an epiphany of dreams. A sort of commentary on Hades, by the Prince of Darkness. Haughtily, condescendingly, the enthralling roar of the organ celebrated this victory over nature. From the masterful way the organist imposed his visions, one could imagine his face: taciturn, with stubborn contours and deep wrinkles, the face of a man experienced in the ways of the world, with not the slightest trace of any ingenuity left. What rich commotion in that music of the devil! Repudiating the laws of Palestrinian impassivity, it went from one immoderate extreme to another in ecstatic or disturbing vocalization, evocative of paradisiacal lasciviousness, of rain and sunshine out of season, of tight-woven cloths impregnated with scents. Sacred music, church music, music down on its knees no doubt, but not before the Creator—kneeling before his creature instead and blissfully fingering the charms of langorous human mammals. *Ad te omnis caro veniet.* A sonorous melodic line, distinct from the intertwining rhythms, applied itself to articulating every nuance voluptuously, handling every note from all sides without neglecting any of its resonance. With consummate mastery of the effects of counterpoint, Niccolo dei Tolomei used his

102

two hands to render the most contrasting sentiments of our ambiguous nature; a lamento in a low register unceasingly accompanied the violent accents of the counter-tenor fanfares, and this lamento using long notes, interrupted here and there by despairing pauses and dissonances, retained an air of litany, poignantly contrite—the contrition of an apostate angel who, caught between the fire of his desires and the recollection of his original peace, is unable to savor his triumphs without at the same time pleading to be forgiven for them.

Long had Pia's husband been playing his tumultuous heart in this way in the most holy, most wise, most Tuscan parish of San Stefano's, before the night came sparkling to the deserted parvis. . .

"I repeat, sir, you are a customer and I must not debauch you—I repeat to you, sir, the Tuscans are demons! They're not born the way other people are, from their mother's womb but, instead, from the belly of the night; son of nobody. Their hands are burning hot, their flesh is seditious. Their skin is so ardent that they spend their time getting undressed. A Tuscan, sir, is a man who gets undressed several times a day; and since the Tuscan women do just the same, you can draw the conclusion that there's one species at least that's not about to become extinct. Some of them are aflame to such an extent that you can see them racing alongside the walls, shedding their cloths as they run, for fear of being late. Where are you running, Tuscan? To the fire of love, brother! No, to the fire of your damnation, you miserable arsonist! Bring your French women here, sir, and if you'll pardon me, they'll find they've become pregant from having walked along the Lungarno Reggio just once between dusk and dark, 'twixt dog and wolf' so to speak (by which I mean, between Tuscans and Tuscans).''

"You are merciless, Andria."

"And what about them—who do they have mercy on? If you stayed in Pisa a few weeks longer, you'd learn that mercy is a sentiment that is not worth anything here. Just you try making one gesture that could be interpreted as charitable—like giving a lump of sugar to a stray dog—and you'll see their smile dissect you from top to bottom and right to left. The dog himself, if he is a Tuscan, will express his gratitude by biting you. . ."

The maître d'hôtel had hardly finished his vehement tirade when Chiarina came in and, without greeting him, went hastily to give Pia's letter to the Frenchman, who was so overjoyed at seeing her again that he kissed her. On the envelope was his name, nothing else. But he felt as if someone had called him. He made as if to go out, then changed his mind and stood motionless, so visibly thinking of some scene he had already lived that Chiarina seemed to remember it herself. She felt a sort of fear, appeared anxious not to linger, and went out. While the Frenchman read the very brief letter, Andria, for his part, continued to look side-long after the maidservant; for lengthy experience of hotel lobbies had long since enlightened him as to the type of messages carried by this kind of furtive female.

"Good news, Andria, good news! I'll be Tuscan for a few days more. I've been invited to the country."

"Did you notice how impudent she was? Didn't even say hello to me. She's borrowing her master's grand manner. Sir, I'm afraid that is Tuscany the country is worse than the city; there you will find malignancy flowing from its purest source. Here at least one feels protected; there is the police, there are people who come and go, there are foreigners; in town the Pisans wear a mask of politeness; they don't what any scandal. But in the country things are different, believe me. There the Tuscans are among themselves, so they do as they like; and fierce they are, too. Keep your eyes open, sir, once you have gone out the gates of Pisa. I'll go with you, if you wish. The season is just about over and I've got some time coming to me; the management will be nice and give me a few days off."

"Come, come, Andria, your horror stories will dissolve in the glass of good wine that we're going to drink together right now. What a hot-blooded, laughing young lady you must be hiding out there in the countryside! since you take so much trouble to forbid me to go that way just when you are planning to slip away there yourself. Out with the truth, Andria: confess you've been bewitched by some pretty peasant whose husband may very well make you hear bells with his blunderbuss one of these days soon. Is it Signorina Chiarina who's put you in a bad mood?"

"I do not have the same reasons as you, sir, to make eyes at Chiarina, and I see she's getting ready to lead you into the country, as they say; so, I am informing you about the country. A hotel, sir, especially a hotel like ours, the richest one in Pisa, is a drawing room where all the smart people are to be seen, with their fancy clothes, their laces, their disdainful smirks and their ties imported from Bond Street. We know them by heart, we do, those perfumed high-society gentlemen. Their wives we know a great deal less; they hide them or take them, but only under escort, to evening parties or the theater. On Sundays, at mass, there is a priest responsible for counting them when they go in and when they come out, for fear someone will snatch them away from them. There's not a single chambermaid but what has been instructed to spy on her mistress. I suppose that Chiarina of yours, like the others. . . Once again, sir, the north and the south are two different things, France is not Tuscany, a spade is a spade, a Tuscan is a deceiver, and Chiarina is a charming young lady whose master is a Tuscan."

"Your scandalmongering will get you into trouble, Andria."

"Quite the contrary, sir; if I didn't go in for slander, the management would have fired me long ago; I am paid to get things off my chest. Otherwise I would be bored. We barkeeps are the equivalent of the kings' fools in the old days. The manager of the Nettuno, a pure Tuscan himself, takes great pleasure in hearing how a fool from Sardinia judges the fools of Tuscany. Now don't go thinking they don't claw and scratch their own compatriots; you'd be mistaken. And where do you suppose I took lessons in paying them back for their own perfidiousness? Why, from them, of course."

"And what a star pupil you are, Andria! Now just slander away to your heart's content and tell me, who is this master of Chiarina's, this organist named Niccolo, I think. . ."

"I may surprise you, sir, but I've asked myself that very question many and many a time. I remember having seen him often. He is taller and younger than he seemed to me the first time we met, the day we ran into each other at the Porta Nuova: I on foot, he in a light cart with bright red wheels, drawn by a horse coiffed with a plume, as in the old days. Another time I had a chance to look him over even more closely, during the *Gioco,* when the city council met here at the hotel. He seemed tired, somehow, and his youthfulness was that of a man who has already lived a great deal; he looked steadily at me with blue eyes that were slightly amused, but their amusement was swimming in sadness. In the midst of all those hastily talking men, I was struck by one thing: his voice, a stage actor's voice. You could feel the man was used to giving orders. I also remember his hands, extraordinarily white and long. I remember that one, deep furrow on his forehead, that went on and on until it was lost in his curly hair. You'd have thought he was a cardinal in disguise, but that is not the right comparison; he moved like a wild animal; his body was obviously more agile than his face would lead you to suppose. Aren't you going to ask my why I remember these things so accurately? Because that devil of a man

108

was worth the trouble; he was seductiveness in person, and I was thinking to myself that unapproachable as he appeared, his friendship must be a hard thing to win. I rejoiced over it. His attitude taught those Tuscans of ours (he is doubtless one as well) a thing or two about arrogance, and his presence could not but make the women and the wives of our city more keenly tempted. I rejoiced at the idea that the agitation their quivering wives would be feeling would disturb the bald-pated sleep of our Pisan notables for a long time to come, and all because of this spellbinding, enigmatic Niccolo dei Tolomei. An out-and-out Lucifer. And then, sir, yes, then Lucifer came forward; he stepped out of the circle of distinguished people standing all around him to come right up to the poor maître d'hôtel from Villacidro; and he did it ostensibly, to flout those fine gentlemen, and he talked to me; we talked together; he put his arm around my shoulder, laughing subtly. While we talked, I saw him become transformed, right there in front of me: his hard lips, his hard nose grew softer; dimples came into his cheeks, such inviting dimples that I would have followed him all the way to hell if he'd asked me to."

"There's one at least who is an exception to that Tuscan menagerie of yours," said the Frenchman, getting up to look out the large window at the clammy waters of the Arno. They reminded him of his first evening—inexplicable, complicated, fright mingled with light—in Pia's drawing room and then that galloping horse, that flight after the organ's sudden silence. Until then he had had the impression of acting deliberately, but now he was no longer sure of it. He adored this woman; by her he let himself be distracted from what had been his reasonable occupations. But he had Lucifer as a rival, a Lucifer who could cast spells even over hotel porters. This Tuscan earth positively gave off something contagious that misled his northerner's instincts. He was painfully affected by it. On several occasions he had felt the danger, but the thoughtful politeness with which he had been received had made him forget it. Now an obstinate, overwhelming anxiety was stealing into him again, as if through some hidden passage. Would he have the courage to take a decision? How would he behave if he met Lucifer? No doubt but what one could not snatch away the devil's wife as easily as all that. Especially since, in order to marry the devil, a woman must have some affinity with him. . .Who was Pia? Into what disastrous spell would she lead him? As he watched the riverscape glint green, his love incessantly sought her and thought it spied some sign of her wherever the Tuscan autumn showed its marvelous face; stilted or at a loss, frank or false, how he loved her! How could he ever be separated from her? Wherever she led him, he would go. Hardly had he said this to himself when he recalled Andria's words: "I would have followed him all the way to hell if he'd asked me to."

"The way you talk, Andria, it sounds as though you've sold your soul to this Mylord Lucifer? Has Tuscany bought Sardinia? For how much, pray? For a few compliments, a single wink?"

"I see you are joking, sir, for Sardinia is not for sale; no one would want it. Aside from Villacidro and its good dry wind, what would anyone be wanting on Sardinian soil, I ask you now?"

"I'll soon have a chance to see that Lucifer of yours at last, since I'm extending my stay; I'll let you know what I think of your griffin."

"Perhaps not, sir; he's pretty hard to grasp, a little like the Buffalmaco that people wonder about—did he ever exist? He's here one minute and somewhere else the next. They say he's a frantic woman chaser—that's what they say, but falsehood flourishes here. Niccolo doesn't like to be seen. His wife herself doesn't always know where he is. But for you it's a different matter, since he's invited you. Rare and meritorious gesture coming from a savage. It's obvious he wants to do you honor. Be ready for anything even so—like for instance hearing the servant tell you when you arrive, 'There's no one, home.' Simply because meanwhile he will have taken it into his head to go hunting, or to do something else; and just as you are about to grumble about how careless he is and swear he can go to the devil, right then, suddenly, he may very well turn up."

And saying this, Andria laughed and laughed, slapping the back of an armchair, mimicking the Frenchman's astonishment and at the same time Niccolo's sarcastic calmness.

But it was growing late in the afternoon, and Andria and the Frenchman did not talk any more that day. . .

7

Into this isolated chamber, seasons and sounds did not penetrate, so heavy and tight-fitting were the doors. Only the light entered it amply, through the high windows. It was their prison of love, their theatre of love. When Niccolo had come up the spiral stairs a little while ago, Cipriana was naked. "Oh, Niccolo, my dear demon! I've been waiting for you for two days; I nearly went out of my mind. Where were you? My one desire, my only love, my dream. Come closer, take me, touch me, I'm dying to have you touch me. What do you want? What can I do for you? Look at me: do you like me?" And he gazed at her, pale with rapture. At the tip of each breast, she had a remarkable brown shadow; her dilated eyes seemed to have lost their pupils. She was animated by an inner tide that gave off a deep odor of veins, raising her toward him imploringly. His expert

hands gripped her by the armpits with the feline grace-
fulness of men sure of being seductive. The kiss he gave
her elicited a long moan, while tears pearled on the
fringe of her lashes. Blond, promising body, sturdy in its
halo of gold, face covered with dream, lips capable in
themselves of creating an art of voluptuousness: accustomed though he was to adultery, Niccolo was stirred
by the confidence of so adorably young a mistress. He
did not take his eyes off the metamorphosis that was
occurring in her, because of him. The silence grew very
soft; he was eager to employ the talents of his inimitable
savoir-faire which urged him to the pleasure of the
moment through a taste for the perpetuity of pleasure.
He had no other god on earth than the thirst he felt for
visions, for slightly barbaric inventions when in a
woman's arms; to women he was always linked by an
ardent union, but never by intimacy. Standing on the
tips of her toes, her back arched in expectation,
Cipriana made the air alive around her; a consummate
musician, he imagined he could already hear surging
from this impatient body the music it concealed.

"*Sola, sola,*" he murmured.

Then on the great green bed, he possessed this beautiful recumbent force, he was possessed by it lengthily,
avidly, seeking here and there an additional lust that

114

might have escaped his experience, trying to penetrate this feminine anatomy to the very bone structure, so as to lose himself in the secret of its labyrinth, to arrive at last at that hoped-for dawn of deliverance that he had guessed, glimpsed at times but never reached. Through the flesh does one attain unto the spirit? Over Cipriana stretched lengthwise across the bed spread that sort of diffuse smile which nature places on the harvested countryside. The texture of her profile was interwoven with another texture: that of the ancient times which Niccolo regretted, when his ancestors frequented the voluptuous monasteries the poet Navagero speaks of, peopled by novices with abundant curls and bared breasts, as was the custom. She quivered plaintively as she breathed, the edge of the lips haughtily, laughingly raised, while Niccolo's hand, moving back and forth from nape to heels, kept the fine web of muscles alert; a faun on the watch, he savored the effects of voluptuousness all along limbs whose every fiber, having feverishly burst, now sought to recover its vigor, and in this return to restfulness found a pleasure by no means inferior to that which had overwhelmed it.

"*Viemmi voglia d'esser morta.*"

After that last whisper, she became voiceless, a statue, docile under the man's hands. She no longer existed.

115

Little by little, the chamber with its white walls, its white ceiling, lighted uniformly by a light which, instead of casting shadows, was cruelly geometrical, had grown de-humanized. Even the bedspread falling onto the floor seemed unreal, each stitch of the cloth riveted with a mineral sheen; rugs and cushions were as if crushed by the weight of their patterns and braids, some of which imitated the adornments of chasubles. No decoration other than a small column supporting a god Pan with amethyst eyes and, on the wall above the bed, a picture of a medieval battle where one would have looked in vain for a man or a face. Nothing but enormous horses, rearing on their hind legs as if climbing, polished armour moving noisily amid flags and broken lances, branches of orange trees whose wrought-iron leaves beat time as the horsemen passed. The oranges that riddled the copse like oil drums, the cabochons that studded harness, the bosses of the bits, the roundnesses of the shoulder-pieces and elbow-pieces in violent colors of gold and night were carried away by the agitation of the battle in the whirlwind of a boreal light. It looked like dancing stars caught in a sublunar storm. Nowhere was there a human feeling of even a heartbeat visible. An unnatural world rearing in solitude; not one real tree, not one glimpse of water, not a scrap of aerial space, nor the fearful vulner-

116

ability of the least animal. Niccolo's chamber of love was saturated with the glacial art of a mechanical battle. Love exhausted itself here, became petrified in a pointless interplay of ligaments and muscles. No dawn rose at the summit of so many sighs, only the muddy top of one of those sun-baked Tuscan hills that you see between Gabellino and Volterra.

"Viemmi voglia d'esser morta." repeated Cipriana, in a voice that was barely perceptible this time. But the man still would not let her go; with a sort of hunger he devoured her soul, anxious that enough of it should remain to satisfy the insatiable desire to feast on this marvelously offered life. She was nothing more than perspiration, bruised legs, bloodless lips; a little more and she would exist no longer, the surface and the derma of her skin being nothing but a gaping wound where the ruthless lover drew long draughts of what had been Cipriana. How could she escape? The door was closed, the walls sealed off; the windows, mere skylights, did not open; isolated on the top floor of a discreet house, this chamber, like some inaccessible dovecote, isolated them from the city. For an instant, Cipriana took her lover's head in her palms to read in it a victory at least: in the depths of his eyes she saw nothing but a corridor of sadness with pleasure fleeing

at the end of it. She had just time to tell herself that from now on she could no longer separate Niccolo from her own blood before she sank into an abyss where her fall became confused with the stopping of time.

In Pisa, at this hour of the day, the gardens start going brown but here, under the glass panes, the light has hidden its last gleams. Cipriana has awakened; for the first time she seems to notice the painting of the battle on the wall and she starts in fear, but not for long, for she knows that she is not in a strange place; there is no reason for her to feel bewildered. If she continues to feel astonished in spite of everything, that is because she has just discovered the silimarity between the riders in the battle and her own rider, her demon Niccolo. She aches from having been trampled by those cavalry squadrons whose hoofbeats survive in her ears; one of those iron men, doubtless the leader with his scarlet cloak, must have swung her up over the crupper to save her; she remembers having panted while her breasts were crushed against the rivets of the armour to which her bare body clung, legs open and head thrown back. She fell, even so, and was gathered up again; a second time she fell and was gathered up once more; now at last she is safe; she opens her eyes wide and can see for herself, beyond the shadow of a doubt, that the battle has ended. The horses are still there, flat in their frame but motionless and fresh; the warriors are frozen in a truce which they are not about to break; only one soldier is dead: he lies belly downward on the ground, ignored by all. At the top, on the right, a grass-edged path disappears in the fields; it looks as through it is snowing.

Cipriana wakes up and her stomach is cold against the shaggy counterpane; around her the white light of the Pisan autumn rains down. Niccolo at her side, his eyes half-closed, has laid his robust hand in the hollow of her back. In this position the two of them offer a study of the nude enhanced by the starkness of the setting. But something is missing; what is it? Cipriana, in fact, feels that someone is missing, instead; who can it be? But no, here is that someone, coming in; she has the slanting oriental gaze that all Pisa envies her. Only Cipriana, because she is dreaming, has seen her come in; perhaps she has been there, secretly present, for some time already; Niccolo is not thinking of Pia and so does not notice her. Pia radiates from her whole person something rustic and airy; in this stifling room she has a fragrance of apple trees or green poplars.

"Get up, Niccolo, your wife is here."

And Niccolo, who knows Cipriana's obsessions and

her mania for creating dangers for herself, calms her with a very specific caress. She protests, sits up and winds her arms around him. She tells him:

"You are my lord on earth, I do not even raise my eyes to heaven any more; I dare not take the time to breathe for fear of being distracted, even for a second, from you. The time passes so quickly that you make me grow old, did you know that?"

He doesn't answer.

She continues:

"One day I will really die in your arms, without your even noticing it; I won't say no. I don't need a soul any more since you have opened a heaven to me; I will withdraw into it, you will put me to sleep there. As you told me this summer, you will place on my head the crown of crowns. Protected by you, I'm not even afraid of God any more. Loving you cannot be a sin. Why, then, should we live always in hiding? You are my king, but our kingdom has no windows; look at it; a bed, four walls and this roof in a district where I cannot come without trembling."

He answers:

"In the open air I would cease to be your demon. Have you ever heard of a demon who was not enveloped in darkness? A demon has a paradise that is discreet,

120

discreet but overpopulated: everybody runs after him. But I—I have only you in my paradise."

She retorts:

"Dear liar, how you mock! In that paradise there is also your tender wife, whom you wedded in the sight of God and the priest. Remember your promise."

A cold smile:

"What did I promise you?"

Pouting:

"That for the time being I am your secret fiancée but that soon I will be the queen of Pisa with a carriage, and pearls, and farmers. You promised me that Pia would go. . ."

The two lovers' voices are lost in teasing kisses, then the man resumes, very low,

"That would not make our celebrations more magnificent."

Between the offered breasts, where a little while ago the throbbing of the artery placed beads of perspiration, Niccolo deposits a kiss that is never ending.

"Even so you are not my heart's neighbor," she says, placing her large bare hand on her lover's hair; "how I would like to tame you so I wouldn't have to cry any more each time you leave me. It seems to me you should understand that; if you do not, who could? I will become only what your love makes of me; is there any power on earth stronger than yours? A minute ago, when you were embracing me, I felt my soul departing from me; and where was it going, if not toward you? And now I am not sure it has come back."

"Did you know that there were three Mary's connected with our Lord? First, the Mother, an austere, archaic person; she must have been from the North. Then, the sister of Lazarus, dreamy, a contemplative. But it was the third one, Mary Magdalene, who had the best role, since she alone was present on the day of the resurrection and the glory; she was the witness of Easter, the Sunday woman, so to speak. Darling Cipriana, instead of being my everyday wife, why wouldn't you be my Sunday wife?"

"Saint Niccolo! Christ Niccolo! What would I do the rest of the time? Oh, I couldn't! But to take your arm and walk through the streets—what a joy that would be. I would have the whole world as a present, as filled with fragrance as the stairway of the Trinitá dei Monti. I will say to you: look at that one, look at this one; let's stop in front of this shop, let's go in and sit at that table, let's go to the sea. Each day time will be reborn in us. You won't believe how much I will belong to you!"

"Perhaps in that case you will be so close to me that I

won't see you any more. Compare the happiness of the poor docile matrons of Pisa with the happiness of those recluses of insane love—Isabella Orsini, or Francesca Polenta, or Vittoria Accoramboni. Because love is not a question of habit; love is waiting for the man who will bring you women a few seconds of folly. I am your folly, Cipriana, I am your sin—two things that are cherished above all else."

Cloistered, occult chamber, bodies ramified in exhausting sensations, hand in hand they watch the sky melt among the swallows, turn color, spread harvested fields with highlights of white here and there; clouds as motionless as milestones, pedestals awaiting their pilasters, foam outlined in light. Tuscany does not exist only in its sites and its arts; it is also on high, among the clouds. Just now, because it is autumn and because evening is not far off, there are slow rivers in the Pisan sky, admirable, drawn with black stone, encircling squat towers, then springs emerging from the west, then a city suddenly thronged with people, and animals moving through it. Cipriana, attentive now, sees that a purple rose bush has emerged in front of a spindle-tree hedge in which irregular winds, here and there, stir fires. She points it out to Niccolo but he thinks he sees fans there instead, opening and closing as they pass from hand to

123

hand.

"I cannot see the three Marys," Cipriana says, ironically.

"Of course not; it would be surprising if you did. All three of them remained on earth, or under the earth, as you like."

Onto the green bed where their bodies joined as one weighed so heavily, the light descending from the skylight throws the ample shroud of the reclining dead.

"Will we never have more than a scrap of sky above our love, captive between these four walls? To reach the paradise of all men and women, is there no other stepladder than this bed? As time goes by we will feel more and more cramped in it. Your mouth, so hot on my mouth today, will begin to sigh for some more appetizing affair. I may be willing to lose my soul with you for hours on end, but how could I say goodbye to my soul forever?"

"Your soul? But do you have a soul, sweet Cipriana? When my dog Sigismondo died, I'd have given all the souls in my house to save him—all but mine, since I don't believe I have one; and even so, it wouldn't have done any good. I'm ready to give up all the souls on this earth, for your mouth and the color of your eyes. Lose your soul? How can you dream of such a thing? You

124

might just as well be deprived of your blood, or your voice, or the curve of your legs; your soul is nothing more nor less than that. I love your 'soul,' Cipriana! Give me a kiss, Cipriana, give me your 'soul'!"

Cipriana hardly has time to consider how sound this impassioned reasoning is before the tempter seizes her. Tomorrow the whole length of her arms and legs will bear parallel marks where she has been bitten, like the hachures which the sculptor's chisel leaves on the statue's body. . .

"At night fall I will leave."

"Your promise, Niccolo, your promise. I am not letting you get out of your promise. If you make no effort to keep me, will I make any effort to be faithful to you?"

"You are my pleasure, and I cannot live without pleasure; you are my instant, but an instant is no small thing; let the heart stop beating for just one instant, and they'll see! all those people who speak disparagingly about instants. Yes, you will belong to me alone."

"How many times, to how many different women, have you repeated this flattering song?"

"Yes, you must belong only to me. Pia will go away. In the country, near the sea, we have some property, a house perched way up high that I've had restored—and

125

there she can dream as much as she pleases. . ."

"It's true then? I will have the carriage, and the horses? I will be seen in public with you? I will not be just a sultana any more?"

"Why not?"

Doubtless there was a tinge of mockery in his skeptical exclamation, but she thought he felt genuine satisfaction at speaking those words at last.

He meanwhile had begun mentally retracing the contours of Pia's face. One more woman that he had slowly subjugated, then made desperate. One more. Who was to blame? They ran after him, threw themselves on him, implored his adoration, underwent his love to the point of martyrdom; then, disillusioned at having failed to shape him in their own image, they deluded themselves into thinking they could go on having the benefit of his generosity while bestowing their hearts on someone else.

"Pia, Pia, why did you betray me? Just think of what we would have built, together. You talked to me about how young you were, and I told you you would be the queen of the territories of Orvieto and Pisa. Will you ever know what extremities of inhumanity I went to, for your sake? When Kristine Daae disappeared, for instance? I will never be a real husband for anybody. I imagined you were coming to me to take me as I was, but no: as far back as I can remember, though your hands continued to grow warm in my hands, your heart grew cold. That is how you all are, you women! You, Pia, have vilified the things in me which conquered you; once your beauty had blossomed, thanks to me, once it had been enriched and confirmed, thanks to me, you used it to attract idiotic foreigners!"

How he had loved her! In his thoughts remained so many images of her: Pia before the window, playing *"La fanfare de la main gauche"* by Muzio Clementi; Pia with a very heavy bundle on back of her head: her mass of hair; she is dark, very dark, and you notice it especially when the sun is shining, as when she is in that very pose, of an afternoon, at the *cascine* of San Rossore.

Chiarina had told him everything: the meetings by the Atlantic, the Frenchman wearing his heart on his sleeve, the way Pia sighed. He had authorized this invitation to Pisa; he had fostered the tête-à-tête on which the sly Chiarina had managed to eavesdrop. "What a faithful wife you have, sir; the gallant was wasting his time," she had revealed. Since then there had been that letter Pia had sent to the Frenchman, the rendez-vous she had just given him. There was an end to illusion. He had not thought things would happen that way again. Perhaps it was inevitable, after all; he was sentenced to solitude without respite, and there was nothing more to be done about it.

"You look at the sky, Cipriana, but I, sweet Jesus! I'm looking for the earth, the heavy flesh of the earth."

"Yet the sky is so lovely when the wind is right in the sunny day. No more prison for Cipriana. A bit of sky from time to time, my God, how good that feels! When we are married, we will have our seasons: my nights will be for you, my days for society."

It seemed to him he had already heard those words in someone else's mouth. "Pia, Pia, why hast thou forsaken me?"

The vespertine hour was enchanting. Any moment now Niccolo would go away, abandoning Cipriana to her joy, her lassitude, her melancholy. Of the day when she would be close to Niccolo at last, she knew that another woman would have to withdraw from him forever, to leave room for her.

"And what if, by some mischance, you were to forget me?"

"One word from you, and I would come back to you."

"What word?"

"Or if not a word, then a sign."

"What sign?"

"Your closed eyes."

"Then I would not see you any more."

"It is the others that you won't see any more, for I—I shall be inside your solitude, behind your eyelids."

"I am afraid of solitude, afraid of tears."

"Don't be afraid; in my heart I will close up your sobs."

"My love, my lover, tell me again that I am right to prefer you."

"Through you, my kingdom is of this world. How could I give up my kingdom? Goodbye for this evening. Everything will soon be as you want it."

"Take me away out of this prison now, right away. Pray God your good resolutions will not weaken. That would be worse than if I died. Take me away."

"Where to, little Cipriana? I am your prison as much as you are mine."

"What if you took pity on her? What if you kept her, out of respect. . ."

"Respect for what? The first thing to do is keep our pleasure safe, spare ourselves any suffering. Who has ever had pity for me? Our pleasure is what counts, Cipriana, only our pleasure."

"Niccolo, I do not know anything about life as yet, but so much sadness shelters in your eyes, and on your lips so little joy, even when you smile, that I wonder how you have come to feel such bitterness. Who hurt you so one day? Who will cure you, my fine foe?"

"What kind of thoughts are you thinking? Why think at all? I don't need to be cured; I'm not sick, not in the least. What dark thoughts on your face! Why think of tomorrow? *Chi vuol essere lieto sia, del doman non v'é certezza* (let him be happy who wishes to, for of tomorrow we have no certainty). Our grandparents used to preach that, way back."

He was leaving. Cipriana was on the verge of crying, but she felt the tears come without anguish or rebellion.

He embraced her so considerately that a wave of charity for him suddenly surged within her. But Niccolo's profile remained hard. She was not unpleased, for she interpreted this as an assurance that he would rid himself ruthlessly of Pia.

8

Isidoro Falchi was happy. Most trusted servant of a master to whom he was superstitiously devoted, he was all the more greedy for his compliments because they were as rare as they were laconic. Now just that morning, Niccolo had praised him for the diligence with which he had set about restoring the old shepherd's cottage at Follonica. And Isidoro glowed with satisfaction. Although he was unaware of Cipriana's very existence, he was not lacking in spitefulness, and he naturally drew parallels between the circumstances today and the circumstances on that former occasion when he had been given similar orders to arrange the house at Follonica. But at that time he had known why and for whom. This time he was puzzled. Of course, his suppositions were taking shape to such an extent that he was almost certain he had guessed the name of the next

131

inhabitant of the shepherd's cottage. A matter involving women, like so many others. Isidoro had been brought up to respect the conjugal code, and here and there he had learned about the mishaps—although doubtless light had never been shed on them completely—which had befallen guilty wives.

This time there must be an explanation; everything must hang together even if the paths of destiny were hidden for the time being from Isidoro's vigilant eyes. Everything did hang together: Pia's anxiety, Niccolo's comings and goings, Chiarina's errands and the sudden, unexplained arrival of this visiting Frenchman; and where the Frenchman was concerned, Isidoro would not have long to wait for enlightenment. The Frenchman was expected at Vetulonia. The master had just summoned Isidoro about that this very morning and, after complimenting him on the work at Follonica, had taken his arm familiarly:

"You remember the Frenchman we've invited, don't you? You must have seen him in Pisa. He will be coming through our part of the country tomorrow; he is to stop over in Vetulonia; he is liable to get lost; he doesn't know anyone there. Get down there early, introduce yourself, offer to guide him to where he will tell you to take him; obey him, you will see; we will all see then,

132

very clearly. And above all, do not be surprised by anything, Isidoro. You will be rewarded, my good friend. I think I know where his own steps and you will lead him. You see, Isidoro, the charm of life is that it is always in motion and never varies."

The day after tomorrow, then, Isidoro would be at the appointed place in Vetulonia, and the Frenchman as well. What would happen there, Niccolo seemed to be guessing very accurately; perhaps he had arranged things himself, with his customary skill. What a stage manager this Niccolo was! What an honor it was to serve him!

"Guess, Andria, just guess where I'm going tomorrow!" joyously exclaimed the Frenchman as he finished his dinner in the Nettuno restaurant, among the empty tables.

"Some place where you will surely not be needing me, sir."

"I'm going all the way to Vetulonia. Do you know that part of the country and how to reach it?"

"A wasteland, sir, moors and tombs everywhere, chestnuts and wolves; none but the devil can keep his appointments in Vetulonia. Remember what I was telling you, sir. You have to learn to howl before setting foot in Vetulonia; and you must also become hard as flint if you're to get into it because everything in

Vetulonia is stone, believe me, I'm not exaggerating: the trees are stones, the souls are stones; the sky itself is made of some substance that the sun cannot penetrate. Which is why the earth never sees it. And why the people there give you an impression that they are constantly on the lookout, waiting for something. They are simply waiting for daylight, and they're liable to wait a long time for it, wait until they die—and even then they're not sure of seeing it. But for the love of God, what will you eat? Pebbles? It would be a sin to let you leave for Vetulonia by yourself; allow me to accompany you, will you?"

"You're joking, Andria. Just tell me how I get to this inferno."

"The train from Livorno to Orbetello won't do you much good. Instead take the country highway inland, that goes from Cascina to Empoli; turn off to the right, toward Volterra, Pomarance, Larderello, Valpiana; from there, take the causeway to Grosseto; a dirt road on your right leads to Vetulonia, and stops there. It is a dead end, at the end of the world; beyond that, I know nothing."

In her letter, Pia herself had advised him not to take the car beyond Vetulonia, as the roads were not passable, after that point. From there he would have to

their long linear nudity and their medieval arrangement, impose their personality on the people, obliging them to build their houses in grovelike shapes and along lines which do not hinder the freedom of the branches; you have only to see how, on certain summer days, and depending on the hour of the day, the trees move about within an area marked off by mysterious landmarks, looking for their exact location, with just enough discretion so as not to frighten the other creatures; and they have been doing this so far as we know ever since a painter named Piero suggested that arrangement to them, in the days of Pope Eugene IV. Gubbio, Empoli and Siena, on the other hand, are dedicated to the zoological kingdom, which explains the extraordinary way the beasts swarm and their cries echo in the Siennese frescoes. But from Volterra to Valpiana and Vetulonia the mineral kingdom triumphs. The very colors become architectural material; the houses are like hills, indestructible, standing steep and wild and unposed against the sky; and those which have not been finished or one of whose walls is crumbling look even more convincing than the others. Built of the famed *pietra serena,* their bony whiteness makes them bigger. Schistose faces with agate eyes appear in the windows. The rivers roll along more pebbles than water. Whereas everywhere else a loving sun swathes glorious Tuscany, here, between Volterra and Vetulonia, the sky is a dark field, walled in sandstone, like the inhabitants and the plants. The light sleeps there, being merely an emanation of the shade. And to that shade herds of things and invisible shapes come to drink, so that, even at noon, in Vetulonia, there is an overriding impression of dusk of which the people are fully aware. They live below the sun, so to speak, not inside it, like fish which, doomed to the shadowiness of the sea, are ignorant of the light above them. In Volterra but also all along the Era, the Cecina, the Bruna or the Ombrone, death is visible, as it were; vivid as it makes the things of eternity, so it makes fleeting cares absurd. The land is prepared for the other world.

Not with impunity does one go through the Tuscan towns when one is not Tuscan oneself. The Frenchman was startled to hear, mingled with the moaning wind in the parched ravines, the voice, the cry of the woman he loved. He was beginning to feel terribly foreign to this country. In Pisa, a fashionable city, he had had the illusion of an affable Italy; here the celebration was coming to an end. Proud, withdrawn and stubborn, enclosed in its own law, the country barred its door to whoever was not one of its intimates. The Frenchman remembered

Andria's advice and was sorry he had scorned it. But
how could he turn back? After the village of Pomarance,
on the road for Massa Maritima, great clumps of chestnuts volleyed back and forth a wind so cold that he
imagined he was on the shores of the Atlantic:

"I have found you at last. . ."

"You do not know me."

"I will continue to look for you."

"You have no right to."

"Be still; give me your lips."

That was the first time. There had been a second
time, when behind the traits of the woman beloved, he
had caught sight of the little girl with the goldfinch,
showing him the diamond wedding band she wore on
her finger:

"Do you believe in hell? I do. The man who comes
near me will touch hell; so leave me, leave before I do
you a great deal of harm."

What would the third meeting with Pia be like? A
treasure amassed by the centuries in this Tuscan land,
she had inherited the terrible beauty of it; she dwelt in a
world whose austerity governed her; here she would
never be alone, impregnated as she was with the essence
of the land, of its sky and its original waters. How
would she fit into the northern land of France, where

there was nothing to correspond to her?

"I know all that or have guessed it, my love, but I want you as you are, you and your country; you will not be mine; it is I who will belong to you as to a new country. In France you will be to me an island planted with grass and with Tuscan olive trees, haunted by the birds who drink of the Era."

And Niccolo? It was about time he thought of that; why hadn't he realized earlier that to take a woman away from her husband was no easy feat in Tuscany? Was Niccolo really as unaware as he seemed of Pia's temptations? Although he did not try to read the mind of a person whom he did not know, the Frenchman felt, judging from the details of certain memories, that there was still no reassuring explanation for many of this Niccolo's attitudes. The more he thought about it, the more images of anxiety went by, above the dizzying images of his passion for Pia. The landscape shut him within its authoritarian domination, blotting out one by one the promises he had thought within his reach, whereas he had merely glimpsed and hailed them from a distance; around his exaltation tightened the stone matrix of all those sovereign wills which composed the soul of Tuscany and of which Niccolo seemed to him a formidable representative. What was he heading for? In

140

his mind he reread the terms of that letter from Pia, whom he already termed "his fiancée," and this brief evocation momentarily revived his joy.

At Massa Maritima a nasty wind, the *libeccio,* was blowing. Formerly the rich capital of the bishop-princes, then the metroplis of the Garibaldians, the little city accentuated the severity of the region with its walls that bore the seal of the wolf, veritable master of the premises in the fourteenth century, and its frescoes of San Bernardino of Siena, the flagellant monk who was the precursor of Savonarola.

Suddenly, unlikely though it seemed, the country lanes as he drew nearer Valpiana were more crowded than the streets of Massa. Something unusual was happening. The Frenchman's car had to mark time amid women in black who laughed as they trotted by, children streaming past as to a celebration, and men who roared with laughter as they clapped each other's shoulders.

"Greetings, friend!" the Frenchman shouted above the crowd to an isolated peasant.

"Greetings to you too, by San Cerbone," the man replied, rubbing his hands together to warm them. He was wearing a brown corduroy smock with alternately wide and narrow ribbing.

The sky had grown olive green with the coming of evening; the earth, saturated with oxides denoting the presence of ores which had been its former wealth, was reddish, alive with scents of mint and another, still more penetrating fragrance; he wondered if it didn't waft down from the narrow terraces where plums were drying.

Exclamations of "Ho, Cipriano! Ho, Bernardino! Antella! Gilda! Annunziata! Sabatina!" could be heard among the groups, which became shadows under the motionless sky. And they walked and they laughed with sober, deliberate gestures, looking as if they had agreed to act out one of those scenes one sees on the vaulted ceilings of chapter halls in Tuscan towns. Sometimes there was a silence one would not have thought possible, coming from a crowd. And in that silence, one could hear the knell tolling from a belfry, a knell of ten notes of which the fifth, the eighth, and the tenth vibrated longer than the others, sustaining the melody with an irregular rhythm: five, three, two. And the whole back country listened and was still; it must have been this silence which, echoed back to the crowd, made it so abnormally calm. Assembled by the pealing bells of death, the people of Valpiana were hastening blithely toward the city.

"By San Cerbone, I don't understand what's going on," the Frenchman said to himself.

"By San Cerbone, I greet you," repeated the peasant, coming closer to the car to have a better look at this intruder, whose bourgeois suit and hand-hemmed breast pocket handkerchief jarred with the almost military arrangement of the procession. He was very wrinkled, very old, and the whiteness of his face stood out in the rapidly darkening night, where only the cloudless arch of the sky remained lighted.

The Frenchman had stopped his car. The people moved around it peacefully—women with round dimpled chins, men with nazarene beards, their arms raised in dogmatic gestures, little girls loftily staring at this spectator situated outside of their realm, little boys whose clothes, with a grown-up cut to them, gave them a slightly odd appearance—all of this formed a one-voiced world in which the Frenchman felt lost. He was in their midst and at the same time infinitely far away. Just as a tree cannot bear several species of leaves, so this land bore only one species of men, all shaped in the same rock quarry, all built with the same T-square, all part of the same architectonic disposition. Which accounted for the ease with which the cortege moved ahead, coherently, without tumult; and also these people's infalliable knack for dressing in harmony with the soil, in a rough but elegant way. Some of the girls, despite their flat heels and their lack of rouge, were astonishingly superior in beauty to the painted women of the drawing rooms in Pisa; in the night he could see neither the rosiness of their skin nor the color of their eyes; only the vigor of their silhouettes revealed a vitality identical to that of thoroughbred animals, so naturally beautiful that no artifice is needed to set them off. They spoke with their firm country voices:

"Good lord, what nonsense!"

"What's wrong?"

"What good's it going to do him, now the beauty's fled? It's not the bell that's going to give the *innamorata* her virginity back again!"

"Only the ladle knows the cookingpot's troubles."

"Think of it, though, just think of that poor old man whose daughter has been stolen from him, for him, it's just as if she'd been buried."

"You can imagine how well I knew Augustina; Piero too, I spoke to more than once. What I think is funny is that right this minute, in some ferny spot, they're making love to the sound of the bell for the dead, five like the hand, three like you know what, two like two..."

"An old idiot, part of the older generation! If you had to sing a *Kyrie eleison* for every girl that ran away with her sweetheart, all the families around here would have sung themselves hoarse long before this, and we'd have the din of those bells clanging in our ears from New Year's Day to New Year's Eve."

"She was right. She did the right thing to leave that house. *Cambia cielo, cambierai stella.*"

"Your father would not do the same thing, surely."

"Oh, my father!. . ."

Was it all the people thronging around him, or the contrast between this merrymaking and his own preoccupations? For the first time since he had arrived in Tuscany the Frenchman felt something that resembled the fear of ghosts. He clung to the gaze of the old man standing in front of the car and asked him, in his faulty Italian:

"Where are they going?"

"Take me with you and I'll tell you, sir."

They reached the top of a hill from which the first houses of Valpiana could be seen, very near, standing around their fountain, with water gushing from it in jets of white light; the front of the church emerged, with its two towers; an eye in the middle: the clock.

"It's our baker, sir. A boy from the village has eloped

with his daughter and the two turtle doves have run away to get married somewhere nearby. The baker is furious; he went shouting all over the place that his daughter Augustina is dead so far as he's concerned, gave some rascally boys a couple of sequins so they'd go toll the knell, and invited all the local people to the funeral dinner. That's where we're going, sir."

A little woman who had been running behind the car nodded as she caught up with them and made signs that she had been following what they were saying.

"You come too, sir," she said; "the invitation is for everybody."

Now that night had turned the town into a thicket of shadows, the Frenchman could see, down below, a sort of theater swarming with guests who went in and out, slammed doors and moved round and round the fountain. Obstinately, the church remained closed, and with good reason. It was impossible to make out the villagers' shapes, still less their faces. There was nothing but a swirl of black hats and black mantillas.

The knell had stopped tolling. It must be time to sit down to the baker's table.

"Would you ask him if he will have me?"

"Not necessary, dear sir, in his house we make ourselves at home. You will be our guest."

146

"In the midst of these people all of a kind, all of the same family, I'm going to feel like a bit of chaff bound in with a shock of wheat," he thought.

How true that was! The Frenchman experienced a great loneliness at this farcical meal, though the whole village was attending it so as not to offend the unfortunate baker, who was certainly the only one in mourning. No one paid the stranger any attention, except to make room for him at the end of a bench. Some two hundred people were there, lighted by fireplaces roaring from top to bottom of the house. They spoke in low voices, and because their host's face was touched with an ineffable melancholy, they no longer felt like laughing. They had come to have fun; and then, from comparing each other's lives and calculating joys and fiascoes, each one began to think that the baker deserved much sympathy after all. The Tuscans drink little; their exuberance is rather restrained. Gradually the atmosphere in these banquet halls turned dull. They had begun talking about their own affairs again. The Frenchman heard a very young peasant next to him talk about the apples in his garden at Acqua Grossa as if they were children; a woman examined the stone in her ring and dreamily suggested that it might have belonged to the Grand Duke's treasure; she passed it around, and no one denied that a crown was indeed engraved on it. Someone, after asking how long it would take the reservoir to fill with water tonight, got up and went out. Through the wide-open doors, one could see the night face to face; on the four young elms in the square, birds rustled the half-dead leaves as they looked for perches. This universe of Valpiana was definitely, hermetically separated from the rest of mankind and linked only to the night and the stars. There was no room in it for hope, exactly as in paradise; for in paradise, why hope? Was it not completed, created once and for all? Was not everyone's place in it assigned in advance for an unlimited duration? Paradise is the proof that one can only be happy when one no longer has anything to hope for, since one already has everything. Just so in the village of Valpiana: the men, the women and the children have nothing to demand or hope; God is quits with them forever. Everything that is within them will never cease to be there and whatever is not within them is scarcely likely to enter them. There is not even anything to expect; expectation does not play any role; everything is there, for all time; no one else has the right to come there. One realizes that whatever we may possess here on earth comes from an unsolicited gift and that it is impossible for us, through our own efforts alone, to

148

acquire anything whatsoever.

"Anything whatsoever, even Pia," the Frenchman thought as he watched a young woman tie her kerchief in the same, precise way as Pia did; vivacious, long, her hands gushed from the rest of her body, free as birds.

"Tomorrow I will see her; tomorrow, touching the palms of both her hands with my finger, I will tell her: my heart is there."

His heart without a doubt, but what of his hopes? He ought to have listened to Andria, ought not to have left the comfort of Pisa, ought not to have wandered along roads which make one discover countries without hope. Like Pia, the young woman with the kerchief belonged to a country in which, because it was perfect, there were no unforeseen events. What was he going to do in Vetulonia tomorrow? He had a premonition now that hope is a misfortune, that only what is already acquired is good.

"Leave me," she had said, "leave, before I do you a great deal of harm."

But there was also the letter that he was carrying, that he had read and reread, the rendez-vous letter, the letter of love.

"I must leave you, dear sir; old men like me go to bed early and get up early. Thank you for having brought me here, and do not forget Valpiana. You have heard our bell toll the knell: the finest in all Italy. . ."

He was awakened by the braying of the donkeys. More surely than the pangs of love, the donkeys gave this country a voice capable of rousing him. Opening the windows of the Valpiana hotel, where he had just spent the night, the Frenchman saw the great sun on the fields, dim and bluish in their bald woods. The day was starting out serenely, indifferent to people's anxieties. Soon, under the harsh light, the colors and images would become black and white, an exact replica of the effects of the night. In order to reach Pia, he would have to pass through so many shadows and so much indifference that he was almost ready to give up. But nothing had been destroyed yet; nothing was lost. Beyond the foothills, where the breath of morning was raising scattered layers of mist, there was the sea; there was the beach of Castiglione della Pescaia where she had written him that she would be waiting for him.

The Frenchman would long remember the calmness of this day and of the road leading through the dark green woods of trees with indeciduous leaves, in which the scarlet arbutus berries were the only warm notes. Between two glens he thought he saw a shepherd watching him, but surely he was mistaken. The road

150

went down toward the lowlands. The winds spread out, smooth as marble.

"Today or never more," he thought; and it might well be, never more. Soon he would know. On the right, the Tuscan archipelago emerged—Elba, triangular Pianosa, Monte Cristo with its royal game reserve, Giglio, Giannutri the isle of love. It was on Giannutri that the captain Gualtiero Adami and his mistress, Marietta Moschini, had lived, nourished by their solitary voluptuousness. Lines of foam, appearing intermittently, betrayed the presence of water gliding along the shores.

Vetulonia. The Frenchman felt as though he had left a considerable lapse of time behind him, as though he had gone past sentinels to reach the forbidden realm. Pia had advised him to go no farther than Vetulonia by car, to continue on foot to Catiglione della Pescaia, where she would be waiting for him; he must be careful of something and someone, she had added. A small river, a bridge, a chapel surrounded by birds, vegetable gardens directly above paved courtyards, gray façades—this is what Vetulonia looked like. The town must hardly have changed since the long-gone days when Hawkwood, the Scottish condottiere, had ravaged the vicinity.

"Can I help you, sir?" Someone had just stepped away from a group of idle men dressed in corduroy and swinging their legs as they sat on the wall along the ravine. Someone whom the Frenchman did not know. The man was wearing a leather cap and had his hands in his pockets. He was smiling; he was coming closer; he was twirling a bit of straw between his lips. The Frenchman had stopped his car and watched him draw near.

"This is Vetulonia, is it not?"

"Yes, sir, may it please you; one could not be there any more completely than you are now. Can I be of some modest help to you? By Christ himself, what a fine car you have! Have you come a long way?"

"From farther away than I am going, my friend. Who can tell me the way to Castiglione?"

"I'm your man, sir; follow me; I'll take you there since I live there."

The man was laughing now, with peculiar haste. Then he said slowly:

"You going to look at the sea?"

"Perhaps."

"To see someone?"

"Perhaps."

"Unless you've come to see the stud farm, or the ponds at Raspollino?"

"Simply to find out whether the sea hasn't changed places."

"The gentleman is not Italian, as far as I can judge, for he seems not to know that with us, nothing ever changes place, everything is here for all time; and also, the gentleman speaks Italian so gracefully—in a divinely foreign way. Would the gentleman be English?"

The idlers on the wall kept on swinging their legs, careful not to intervene in a dialogue that was of no interest to them. The Frenchman shrugged his shoulders; there in their midst, he was dying with happiness at being so close to Pia but uneasy at finding himself a prisoner of this motionless world.

"Today or never more. Today or never more." Isidoro did not leave him for an instant. He had never been mistaken about other people's weaknessess, and it was obvious that this particular Frenchman was as foolish as only those accursed tourists could be who wander around Italy with full pockets and empty heads. He had never been so close to one before. The sight of him, who so blissfully thought himself worthy of dethroning Niccolo, made him laugh aloud once again; the very idea that Pia could prefer this scatter-brained creature to the magnificent Niccolo made his last illusion about the female of the species collapse. Let her go to the devil! She would merely be getting what she deserved.

As for the Frenchman, he had quickly realized that Isidoro was that mysterious "someone" whom she feared. While the two of them followed the river Bruna downstream as it slowly flowed between the waterlilies, horses noiselessly snorted in the huge spongy meadows whose limp grasses cushioned their galloping gait.

"Be careful where you step, sir; you should not have worn thin shoes, suitable for city wear."

He felt sick at heart now as he walked. Opposite, on the rocky spur that Pia's letter mentioned, he could clearly see what she called "the shepherd's cottage" which looked to him like a ruined farmhouse. Soon he saw the beach, and it made him recall the meeting by the Atlantic, the organ in Pisa, a pair of eyes, those eyes. . .

"Whom are you looking for, sir?"

Isidoro had spoken with a note of triumph which suddenly enlightened the Frenchman. The bell in Valpiana tolled and tolled in his head, ironically, desperately. And then, at the same time, an incomprehensible thing happened: toward the rocky spur, in the shelter of a ridge, those were no longer just horses running but people on horseback, leaning low so as not to be seen; and he was able to make them out only because his eyes were literally devouring every inch of land where Pia might be waiting.

Isidoro had understood instantly. His role had come to an end.

"I will wait for you here," he said, and left the Frenchman to walk on alone through the meadow, cross the last dip in the land that still hid the sea and disappear down the other slope.

She was there. Her shadow was there. At the edge of the beach, three trees, surrounded by an open sky, watched over the calmness of the landscape. Attached to one of them by a chain was the ochre and tar-colored boat against which Pia was leaning. Her face, encircled by a black kerchief, was invisible in this dazzling desolation. Her bare hand, whose fire he had worshipped, was playing with the sand of the sea, a sea so empty that it seemed to be calling someone. He had understood. He had understood that if he took one more step, she was doomed. He dared not make any sign to her, look again more closely at the face he had loved so much and to whose features distance gave a surprising mortuary cast. What was he going to do now with this tenderness which was only for her? What was to become of him? But why ask too much? At least he had known the face of the woman he was to love in this world. Henceforth, thanks to the woman who had made all things beautiful, he would have a pact with the grasses and the animals; the earth would be beautiful everywhere he went. It was in Pisa that he had become what he would be.

He turned back toward Isidoro, who was leaning against an olive tree a-quiver with gray birds and sucking the eternal bit of straw as he waited for him:

"You are alone, sir?" he asked, disappointed.

But in him swelled only, unappeased, unappeasable, his desire that sought and would always seek to join her, her and no other, because only in her did he discover in himself an infinite capacity for feeling.

"You are alone, sir," the servant repeated.

Despite the autumn, the air was still warm on the high sea. He pictured himself there with Pia, like two waves side by side, beyond those who were present, beyond the living.

They headed back toward Vetulonia. Having reached the angle from which the beach was still visible, he could not help turning his eyes: Pia had lifted her head just then, so that he was able, this final time and from very far away, to contemplate together in one image her face, the world and the sea.

While Niccolo and his villagers, sitting tall on their mounts and stiff as justice, watched from the headland of la Castagnola, desperately waiting for the sight of an assignation which did not materialize.

156